Declan Kirby
GAA Star
Away Days

Michael Egan

Gill Books

Gill Books
Hume Avenue
Park West
Dublin 12
www.gillbooks.ie

Gill Books is an imprint of M.H. Gill & Co.

© Michael Egan 2021

978 07171 9050 8

Copy-edited by Emma Dunne
Proofread by Jane Rogers
Printed by CPI Group (UK) Ltd, Croydon, CRO 4YY

This book is typeset in 12 on 18pt Tahoma.
The paper used in this book comes from the wood
pulp of managed forests. For every tree felled, at
least one tree is planted, thereby renewing natural
resources.

A CIP catalogue record for this book is available from
the British Library.
5 4 3 2 1

About the Author

Michael Egan has been a primary school teacher for over ten years and has coached several school GAA teams. He also set up Laois GAA TV, a website that shows highlights of important GAA club games in Laois.

Acknowledgements

The *GAA Star* series is dedicated to all the coaches of Gaelic games throughout Ireland and around the world. Anyone who has played Gaelic games will tell you the many positive benefits you get from playing. The most important thing for children partaking in GAA is that they have fun and get the opportunity to make new friends. Gaelic games are also fantastic for developing social skills, a work ethic, keeping fit and healthy, and helping with the transition to secondary school. It is often an easier transition as, more than likely, a child will know somebody when they go to secondary school through being involved in GAA.

I would like to thank Sarah Liddy, who was the catalyst for these books. I must also thank Catherine Gough and Emma Dunne for their extraordinary hard work and dedication. They gave many useful and insightful recommendations throughout the editing process. Thank you to Bartek Janczak for the page design and to Rob Torrans for the cover illustration. Thanks also to the marketing and publicity team, Teresa Daly, Ellen Monnelly and Avril Cannon. I would also particularly like to thank my brother, James, who assisted with editing and gave many beneficial recommendations.

Thank you to everyone at Gill Books for all that they do.

Contents

Chapter 1

The Phone Call

Ever since Declan Kirby started playing Gaelic football with Smithgreen, he'd dreamed of winning a county final. Now his team had defeated St Saran's and were showing the cup on stage in Smithgreen square in front of the locals. His dream had become a reality.

They would never have won if it hadn't been for their coach, Sam. Declan wanted to thank him for all his hard work, but he barely had time to breathe with all the people coming up non-stop to shake hands and congratulate them.

'Hey, Declan!' He turned to see his best friend, Stewy, waving at him. 'I was just showing off the cup to my neighbours, but I had to stop. It's so heavy!'

'It weighs more than you'd think, doesn't it?' Declan said. 'It all happened so fast I didn't get a chance to say well done to you after the match – you played brilliantly, Stew.'

'You're one to talk! You scored the winning goal. You're the reason we're champions.'

'Ah, sure, everyone played well. Everyone deserves credit,' Declan said, blushing. 'Speaking of which, where's your dad? I want to thank him for everything.' Sam, their coach, was Stewy's dad. Declan knew they wouldn't be here without him.

'Busy doing coach business!' Stewy said. He pointed behind him. 'He's been talking to that guy for a while now.'

Declan looked at where Stewy was pointing. He saw Sam speaking to a man he didn't recognise. The square was quite loud, as everyone was feeling hyper, so Sam was leaning in to listen to what the other man was saying. Sam had his arms crossed and an intense look on his face. It was clearly a very important conversation. When Sam saw Declan looking at him, he turned to shake the man's hand and waved him goodbye before walking towards Declan and Stewy. 'Hiya, lads. You having a good time?'

'Yeah,' Declan said. 'The best!'

Sam whipped out his phone and glanced at the screen. 'Hey, Stewy, we need to make tracks. Get your coat and we'll take off.'

'Already?' Stewy said, confused.

'Don't worry. You'll see your friends again soon.'

'Sam, have you seen Harry?' Declan asked. Harry Buksa was one of their best players, but he was going back to Poland soon, and Declan wanted to make sure he got to say goodbye properly.

Sam gave him a funny look. He was clearly thrown by the question. 'No. See you soon.'

Just then, Declan's dad appeared from the crowd in front of him. 'I think it's a good time for us to go too.'

'Oh, OK,' Declan said, deflated. He'd felt on top of the world a few minutes ago, but now it seemed the celebration was already coming to an end.

'Oh, that reminds me,' Sam said, turning back to him. 'If you're heading home, Dec, you should take the trophy with you.'

He was speechless. 'What? Seriously?'

'Well, somebody has to take it. And you scored the winning goal.'

'Thanks, Sam,' his dad said. 'I'll pick it up and put it in the car. You get your bag, Dec, and I'll meet you in a minute.'

* * *

The next morning, while he was eating breakfast, Declan's mum ran in excitedly with her phone in her hand.

'It's Sam,' she said, pointing to the phone. 'Sounds like he has something important to tell you.'

'Oh, OK,' he said. 'We just saw him yesterday. I wonder why he's calling so early?'

He took her phone and put it to his ear. 'Hey, Sam. What's up?'

'Declan, I want to talk to you about something important. I didn't want to tell you and the lads this news during the celebrations. I wanted to tell each of you separately.'

Sam always tried to sound professional when talking about football, but Declan could hear the excitement in his voice. 'This year, Galway are hosting the inaugural Under-12 All-Ireland competition.'

'Oh, OK,' Declan said, unsure where this was going.

'It will be a knock-out competition, with all county teams involved,' Sam continued. 'At the end of the final, Brendan Kelly came over to me. I don't know if you know who he is? He was the trainer of the county minors for the last two years. Anyway, he's been appointed manager of the county Under-12 team for this year. He's asked for you to go for trials for it, as well as Stewy, Bushy, Big Mike and Brian Bohan. The trials are tomorrow at 10 a.m. It's fantastic news because they are holding an Under-13 competition next month and none of the Smithgreen Under-13 players have been asked to attend trials for it.'

Declan was blown away. They'd only won the cup the day before! He knew he had to make a decision fast, as Brendan Kelly was a big deal. Opportunities like this came once in a lifetime. As he tried to collect his thoughts, his excitement turned to concern. 'That's great, Sam ... but what about Dereck? Or Harry?'

'Sorry, Dec. The X-ray shows that Dereck has broken his ankle. And Harry has already flown back to Warsaw.'

'Really?' It was a shame. Dereck and Harry were their best players.

'The competition is going to be played off over the week of the Ocean Race festival,' Sam explained. 'But it's only being held in Galway up until the semi-finals. The final is going to be in Croke Park.'

The Phone Call

Declan's eyes lit up. Croke Park was the biggest stadium in all of Ireland. It was his dream … no, it was the dream of every young player to play there.

'I'll give it my best shot, Sam,' he replied.

'I know you will,' he said.

As soon as he hung up, Declan ran over to his mum and started to explain everything to her. He was so hyper, she could only understand every other word, but she heard enough to understand what the phone call was about. 'That's wonderful, darling,' she said, hugging him tightly.

'Imagine!' He sighed. 'Actually playing for the county.'

Declan's mum always tried to be a positive role model for her son, and she encouraged him in every aspect of his life. Although she believed he had it in him to be a truly great player, she'd never realised the day would come so early. This was a big opportunity, but she knew it was going to be tough too. She had more than a passing interest in football and knew enough to know Brendan Kelly ran a tight ship and only a handful of players passed his trials. She didn't want Declan to put all his hopes into this county run, knowing the chances of passing were slim. Then again, she'd never thought Smithgreen would win the county final, so perhaps she would be surprised again.

'Well, you know how difficult it is to do that. Just do your best and see what happens. Try to enjoy the experience.'

'Mum, we just won the championship! I scored the winning goal! What could possibly go wrong?'

Chapter 2

Trials

The next morning, Declan's mum gave him a lift out to the county grounds. They arrived at 9.30, which gave him half an hour to get ready and catch up with Stewy and the others. As soon as they entered, he saw a man he didn't recognise at the gate. He was about 20 years old and looked really athletic. He waved to them as they approached.

'Hi, I'm Tim,' he said. 'You must be the guys from Smithgreen. Congratulations on winning the final! Come this way.'

As they walked towards the dressing room, Declan counted over 40 players already there. He'd thought he would be one of the first, since he'd arrived so early, but it looked like he was one of the last. He noticed David Jenkins from St Saran's. It was weird to see him again so soon after they'd played against him in the final. As Declan gazed around, he saw no sign of St Saran's most notorious players, Tommy and Jim Culbert. He hoped they weren't coming. Those guys had been a nightmare during that match. They had no decency or honour. They would do anything to win.

When the Smithgreen boys got to the dressing room, they saw different-coloured bibs on the benches. As they put the bibs and the rest of their gear on, a man walked in. At first, Declan thought it was the same guy they'd seen outside, but this man had a T-shirt that read 'Bainisteoir'. It was the man he'd seen speaking to Sam yesterday. Seeing him up close was weird. He looked like a totally ordinary person. Didn't stand out at all. But in his head, Declan was in the presence of a legend.

'Good morning, everybody,' he said. The dressing room went silent. 'My name's Brendan Kelly. The first thing I would like to say is congratulations to all of you on being selected for the trials. You are all fine footballers but, unfortunately, out of the 45 of you here today only 20 can be selected to represent the Development Squad against some of Ireland's best teams. As you can see, there are four different-coloured bibs. You're going to play two games and then get some lunch while we deliberate. At 4 p.m. this afternoon, the 20 for the panel will be announced.'

Whoa. Declan was starting to get a little anxious. He was so excited about being there that he'd forgotten he mightn't even make the top 20. By four o'clock, his dream of playing in Croke Park could be over. He could feel his nerves acting up and realised he had to shake it off. Panicking wasn't going to help. He had to focus. Do what his mum had said: enjoy it and try his best. They'd just won the championship. He could do this.

Since Declan had a blue bib, he followed the rest of the blue-bib players onto the first pitch. Stewy had an orange bib on, so he would be playing on the second pitch. Since the first two matches would be played at the same time, Declan knew he wouldn't get another chance to speak to him. 'Yo, Stewy!' he shouted.

He spun around. 'Yeah?'

'Best of luck, man,' Declan said. 'Let's show them what we're made of. You can do it!'

'Yeah,' Stewy said with a nod. 'Deffo.'

In the first match, Declan felt he played quite well. He managed to score a goal and a point. He also set up a goal for one of the others. Only one other player on his team scored more, so he felt like he had a chance as long as he could keep up that pace.

In the second match, he scored two points. This time they were up against the team wearing yellow bibs – and Declan was playing against Smithgreen's own Brian Bohan, who played excellently at midfield.

Trials

Declan nearly scored a goal but got tackled – unfairly, he felt – just before he took the shot. It was clear in the second match that some of the players were playing more desperately. They didn't want to be sent home and were relying on cheap tackles to get the ball. Declan felt like Brendan wasn't going to take on players who played unfairly, even when they showed promise. The All-Ireland competition would have really high standards, and he knew they wouldn't put up with that sort of behaviour. He looked over at Brendan and could see him shaking his head. Although the player got the ball off Declan, it was clear Brendan didn't like how he'd done it.

The referee blew the whistle to signal the end of the game and the players were called to gather around Brendan.

'Hey, guys,' he said. 'You all played really well today. I have a lot to think about for the next hour while you go and get something to eat. At four o'clock sharp, make your way to Room 8 where we'll make the announcement.'

The boys walked back towards the dressing room and Stewy gave Declan a high five. 'All we can do now is wait.'

As they made their way to the canteen, Declan could feel his tummy rumbling. And yet, he was so nervous he could barely eat. He imagined most of the players felt the same way.

Stewy gave him a reassuring nudge on the shoulder. 'You played really well – I'm sure you'll make it.'

'Not sure, Stew. Let's see what happens.'

'Hey, a lot of players should feel worried. But not you. I was watching you. You proved that winning goal in the final wasn't a fluke. You have something special.'

'Thanks, Stew. You played really well yourself. I had a look at one of your games when we had a break for a few minutes. Hey, any idea where Hector Hernandez is for these trials? He'd be a sure thing to make this team.'

'Dad said he's visiting some relations in Spain with his family.'

'Well, the team would be much stronger with him on it, but I suppose that leaves an extra space for somebody else.'

As they finished their meals, Tim came in. Although everyone was in the middle of a chat, the whole room fell silent as soon as they saw him. He looked around, making eye contact with all of them. 'Alright, guys. This is the big moment. Follow me.'

Chapter 3

The Announcement

The players followed Tim, and Declan could feel the butterflies in his stomach going crazy. They walked into the room to see Brendan sitting by a table.

As they got settled, Brendan stood up and began to speak. 'Whether you are chosen or not, you've all already had the honour of being selected as the best players for your age in the county. You did yourselves proud with the effort and commitment you gave in the games today. However, as you know, this is a very high standard, and, if chosen today, you will be playing against some of the very best county teams where the standard will be even higher. Some of you will not get the chance this time, but that doesn't mean you should stop trying. Just keep practising and you will get better. And without further ado ...'

He picked up his notepad and started flicking through the pages. In no particular order, Brendan started naming off the players who'd made the panel. 'Michael Kennedy, Billy Graham, David Jenkins, Brian Bohan, Paul Lynch, Stewart O' Neill ...'

The suspense was killing Declan. He didn't make eye contact with anybody. He just stayed in his own headspace. His heart was in his mouth. He grew more nervous after each name was spoken, knowing that his chances of being called were growing less and less.

Then Brendan said the eleventh name: 'Declan Kirby.' And that was it. He was safe. He felt like jumping up and doing handstands, but he kept his cool. He had to remember there were guys who had worked just as hard as him, maybe harder, but they weren't getting this chance.

After Brendan called out the twenty names, he looked up and sighed. 'If I didn't call your name, I'm afraid this is the end of the road for you for now.'

Declan looked up to see tears rolling down the cheeks of some of the other players. It was a shame. Some of them had played really well. There were lots of handshakes and best wishes while the unfortunate members left the room.

But Declan was glad he'd made it through. What made things better was that Stewy and the other Smithgreen boys made the team as well. Stewy didn't score that much but he was lightning fast and created a lot of chances. Bushy had ninja-like reflexes as a goalkeeper so they'd obviously taken note of that. Big Mike and Brian Bohan were known for their stamina and strength, so Declan wasn't surprised they were picked.

The Announcement

'This is how it's going to work, lads,' Brendan said. 'This competition is going to run over a few days. We'll start training tomorrow morning at 10 a.m. It's six days till we head to Galway for the start of the competition and our first match. The draw is being made on Saturday at 11 a.m. Good luck to all of you.'

Chapter 4

Jesse Owens

That evening, Declan's grandfather joined his family for dinner. Being a huge football supporter, he was delighted his grandson had made the team.

'I had a great time playing football myself, Declan,' he said with a cheeky grin, while Declan's parents were dishing up in the kitchen. 'Sport wasn't just fun for me. It was necessary. It makes you feel alive. If I was twenty years younger, I'd probably still be playing! The roar of the crowd, the thrill of scoring a goal, the hope of getting to a final …

'But before I got to play senior football, I was working in the coalmines in England for a few years. As you can imagine, it was quite a dark place to work and I didn't get much time off to practise. So I practised in my head. You've got to visualise, Declan. You've got to see it happening.'

'Yeah, I do that sometimes, but Ms Murphy shouts at me for daydreaming.'

'Well, perhaps school isn't the best place to do it! What are you dreaming about, anyway?'

'I – I picture myself playing in Croke Park.'

'Ah, that takes me back,' his granddad said, gazing upwards.

'Have you played there?' Declan asked.

'Oh heavens, no!' he said, waving his hand. 'But I've watched many games there in my time.'

'Were you there when it opened?'

'It was built in 1884 – I'm not that old, you know!'

'Oh, right,' Declan said. 'Sorry! But you know when it opened, right? So you must know a lot about it.'

'Oh yes. To many people, Croke Park is just a big stadium. That's all they see. But it's not just a building. It's not just a place for footballers and hurlers to have a nice little game. Croker was a beacon of hope back in its time. And it still is. First time I was there was in 1961. My memory isn't what it used to be, but I remember that day like it was yesterday. Down against Offaly. The stadium can hold over 82,000 now. But before they expanded it a few years ago, it could only hold 50,000 – or so we were told.'

'What do you mean?'

'Well, when I was there in '61, there were – and I'm not joking here – over 90,000 people jammed into that place. It was the most people the stadium ever had.'

'Why did so many extra people come?'

'The same reason everyone comes. For the love of the game. So you daydream your heart out, Declan. People only daydream about things they love and what's wrong with that?'

'Yeah, well, I'm pretty sure that even if I explain it like that to my teacher, I'll still get in trouble. Ms Murphy says it's a sign of laziness.'

'Hogwash!' his granddad snapped. 'Daydreaming is important. Sometimes, it's even necessary.'

Declan looked confused. 'How can daydreaming be necessary?'

'Well, let me ask you something,' his granddad whispered, leaning in towards him. 'Have you ever heard of Jesse Owens?'

The name sounded familiar but Declan couldn't picture a face. 'I'm not sure ...'

'The great Olympic athlete?'

'Which Olympics was he in? Recently?'

'In 1936.'

'OK, well then I definitely haven't heard of him.'

'He went on a boat from the US to Germany. He was on that boat for two weeks. He didn't have time to practise so he visualised himself running the race, every step. No one gave that young lad any hope of winning. At that Olympic Games, he walked away with four gold medals.'

Declan's jaw dropped. 'Wow, that's incredible. Do you really think imagining himself winning helped?'

'If you have a bit of talent and you're willing to work hard, anything is possible. Things don't always happen in straight lines – it's how you react to them that matters. Jesse Owens could have lost those races if he didn't have the right way of thinking. He could have made excuses and said it wasn't his fault if he didn't win because he couldn't practise. But he didn't. He found a way around it. He reacted the right way and that reaction made him a champion.

'And you, Declan. You reacted the right way when you didn't make the Smithgreen team the first time you tried. You could have had a tantrum and sulked until you were blue in the face. But you didn't. You got on with it and you showed them why they should have started you in the first place. I suffered my fair share of setbacks throughout my career – injuries, getting sick, not having money. But I never made excuses for it. And neither should you.'

After talking to his granddad for ten minutes, Declan felt like he'd learned more than he had in school all year. Every time he came over, he filled his mind with knowledge.

'So, Granddad, I'm going to be quite busy for the next two weeks. Any advice you can give me?'

His granddad leaned towards him and held out his finger. He always did this when he really wanted to emphasise a point. 'When you're playing as a forward, always make the run even if you don't get the ball. If you make ten runs and get the ball once, that's all you might need to score. Always anticipate the defender making a mistake, because if they do, you're ready to pounce on it and that could make the difference between winning and losing.'

Just then, Declan's mum came out with two plates. 'Alright, who's hungry?'

It sounded like Declan was going to need all the energy he could get if he was going to be at his best over the next two weeks.

'Thanks, Mum. Looks delicious,' he said. 'Maybe I'll even have seconds!'

Chapter 5

The Draw

As the players lined up for the first training session, Brendan made an announcement. 'You are the best players for your age in the county. It's going to be tough to make this team. Everything you do, do it to the best of your ability. What we're looking for here is a good attitude and giving 100 per cent. Listen, learn and try to do what we tell you.'

The training started with some drills and sprints. After that, they played a match. It was obvious from the start that everybody was pulling their weight. Although it was training, everyone was acting like they were playing in a final. Some of the players looked like their lives depended on it. Everyone was sharp and alert. Although Declan thought he played well, it was hard to stand out because the standard was so high.

When the session was finished, Brendan called them over. 'Good work today, guys,' he said. 'On Saturday at 11.00 a.m., they'll be making the draw for the competition. It's going to be an open draw, where any team can be drawn against any other. This is a knock-out competition, lads. There's no qualifier system in place here. Needless to say, I will be in attendance.'

The next morning, Declan convinced Stewy to get the train with him up to Galway to attend the draw. His father reluctantly came with them, using the opportunity to do some work on his laptop and then a bit of sight-seeing around Galway city. The draw was

taking place in a GAA centre beside Pearse
Stadium. The mayor, Devrell O'Shea, was
there and there were even a few cameras. The
competition was a big thing for Galway too, as
many people would be coming to visit.

The mayor and a businessman who was
sponsoring the event were making the draw.
As the mayor walked on stage, he tapped
the microphone to make sure it was working.
'I would like to welcome everyone here
today to the draw of this fantastic underage
championship competition. And without further
ado, we will now pick the first two teams.'

O'Shea turned to his left to face a rotating
drum. The drum was filled with cards labelled
with county names. He spun the drum around
before picking out the first card. He turned to
the microphone and shouted, 'Wicklow.' He
picked out another card and called out, 'Clare.'
Wicklow would be playing Clare.

Declan's county was pulled out next. Stewy
and he glanced at each other, grinning with
excitement. As they waited with bated breath,

the mayor pulled out another card. 'Sligo,' he announced. They would be playing Sligo.

When the mayor finalised all the matches, he made one last announcement. 'As the competition is being held in Galway, they will kick off proceedings in four days' time with their match against Wexford, with more games to be played throughout the day. Thank you for attending the draw and I hope you enjoy the games. If you have some free time, have a look around Galway city. It's one of the most beautiful cities in Ireland.'

Stewy and Declan walked out and high-fived each other. Now they had a game to focus on. After Stewy, Declan and his dad had a burger and a look around the city, they headed home on the train. Stewy and Dec played cards – his dad played one hand but he was tired and soon nodded off. Declan was glad because he often seemed concerned when the boys got overexcited about football. He was afraid too much football might interfere with Declan's schoolwork.

The Draw

Declan then asked Stewy a question that
had been bugging him since they'd left Galway.
'How do you feel about playing against Sligo —
honestly?'

He could see that Stewy was trying to
answer the question and play cards at the
same time but his brain could only focus on
one or the other. After a few seconds, he threw
his cards down. 'Sligo … I mean, we know
they'll probably have a lot of good players.
And Harry and Dereck couldn't even attend the
trials — they would have made the team for
sure and made us way stronger.'

Declan couldn't tell if Stewy was being
negative or realistic — either way, he had a
point. But Declan had to look at the situation
optimistically. Even though they didn't have
Harry and Dereck on this team, there were still
lots of great players on the panel.

But unfortunately, Stewy wasn't finished.

'Dec? We have another problem.'

'Really? What's that?'

Stewy sighed deeply, shaking his head. 'We have to be good enough to make the team.'

Chapter 6

What's in the Box?

Declan took one last look in his bag to make sure he'd packed everything. As he made his way to the bus station, he could feel the excitement welling up inside him. He couldn't wait to spend a few days on the road. But at the same time, he couldn't get ahead of himself. He didn't want to watch the game from the bench. He was determined to make the starting team.

Just then, he felt Stewy nudging his shoulder. 'It's here.'

The bus bringing them to Galway had just arrived at the station. As the door opened, Brendan spoke. 'You are representing your county. Don't forget that for one moment while we are away.'

The first lads on the bus naturally chose to sit at the back, presumably because Brendan was going to sit at the front. The driver, Paddy, was helping to put all the bags away in the huge compartment under the bus. Nearly every player brought something on the bus with them: books, Kindles, headphones, magazines, chocolate.

Declan noticed that Bushy was getting on the bus really slowly. He was moving so carefully, it was like he was made of glass. What was he doing? As he sat alone on one of the double-seats, Declan saw him sneakily pull out a mysterious box, about the size of a shoebox. Whatever it was, he seemed to be protecting it with his life.

As Declan walked by, he couldn't help but say something. 'Hey, Bushy – what's up?'

What's in the Box?

Bushy instantly covered the box with his jacket. 'Eh ... nothing!' he muttered, intentionally avoiding eye contact.

'I can see you've something under your coat. What is it? Go on, let us all in on the big mystery.'

'Yeah, don't keep us in suspense,' Stewy said as he followed behind Declan.

Bushy looked behind him to make sure nobody had heard. He leaned in towards Stewy and Declan. 'Just something I can't afford to lose,' he whispered. 'It'd be of no interest to you at all.'

Stewy took a step forward. 'Now, Bushy. If you say something is of no interest to us at all, you automatically make it ten times more interesting.'

The lads behind them queuing for seats were getting impatient.

'Come on, move on,' Paul Lynch moaned.

'We haven't got all day,' David Jenkins added.

As Declan took his seat beside Stewy, they both looked at each other. 'What do you think Bushy is up to with that box?'

'Yeah, it's like he's guarding secret FBI files!' Stewy said.

It seemed the rest of the team had noticed something was up with Bushy too. As the bus began to fill up, other players passing him bombarded him with questions about his mysterious box. While Bushy was calmly dismissing them, David Jenkins tried to yank it from under his jacket. But as a goalkeeper, Bushy was pretty skilled at keeping things out of people's reach, and held it above his head, away from Jenkins's grasp.

'Fine, keep it then,' David said as he walked on to his seat. 'But I'll find out at some stage what you're hiding!'

'Sure you will, Jenkins!' Bushy laughed. 'Best of luck with that.'

Declan was delighted that Stewy was on the trip too. Things wouldn't have been the same without him. His good humour made him great company and he put that same energy into his performances when playing.

As the bus pulled off, Declan got a text from his mum saying that both she and his

What's in the Box?

dad couldn't wait to see him at the game. He'd presumed he wouldn't see them until the trip was over. He couldn't believe they were going to take time off work and travel all that way to see him play!

Since Declan had some time to kill, he thought he should learn a bit more about his team. 'Hey, Stew. Can you tell me anything about the other players?'

'What do you mean?'

'Well, because your dad is a coach, you always seem to hear bits and bobs about other players. Brendan said Billy Graham will be the captain. What's he like?'

'Billy's sound. He's quiet. Keeps to himself but he's a solid player.'

Any time Stewy was asked about a player, he answered in an instant. It was like his mind was a computer where he'd stored all the data about every player in each team. No matter what player he was asked about, he always had an answer.

'What about that guy there?' Declan said, pointing to the lad in the front seat.

37

'That's Paul Lynch. He's a messer. He and David Jenkins are the clowns of the group. But when they play, those two are dead serious. You saw how good David was in the county final. If he gets the ball near goal, he's almost guaranteed to score. Dad told me Paul is great at making the other players second-guess what he's going to do with the ball. They'll both be good on the team ... so long as they stay out of trouble.'

The more Stewy talked about the players, the more positive Declan felt about the match. He looked around the bus at the boys and it felt like they were a proper team. He thought they'd get bored or tired on the drive, but the lads kept chanting and singing for the whole trip.

When the bus finally stopped, Brendan held his hand up to signal an end to the fun and games. 'Glad to see we're all in such fine spirits, lads. Hope we're still in as good form after our first match.'

Declan looked out the window to see they had arrived at Pearse Stadium. They were

going to be staying overnight in Galway,
regardless of the result. He really hoped they'd
have something to celebrate.

Chapter 7

Benched

Declan had never set foot in Pearse Stadium before. It was 60 years old but had been recently done up, so it looked brand new. A lot of big matches took place there and they took really good care of it. It was an honour to be playing there.

As he made his way to the dressing room, he could see everybody looked tense. Nobody was singing or joking now. If they lost this, there was no second chance. If they lost, they went home. End of story.

Benched

While they were sorting their gear out,
Brendan came in. 'Lads, I just want to say
you have been a credit to yourselves and your
families with the effort you've put in over
the last few days. Of course, some of you
are going to be disappointed. We can't start
everybody. But we all have setbacks in life. It's
how we deal with them that shows our true
character. There are a lot of people here who
think it's just a nice thing to be entered into
the competition. But I've seen enough talent
in you guys in the last few days to know we're
not just another team. You can give Sligo and
all the other teams a run for their money.

'And with that out of the way, let's look at
the team for today. In goals, Adam Frosby.
Right wing-forward, Stewart O'Neill ...'

Declan was barely listening while Brendan
rattled off the list. He was just waiting to hear
his name. He grew more and more impatient
as each one was called out. As Brendan
reached the end of the list, Declan realised
what was going to happen. He wasn't going

to start this time. He was going to be a sub. As Brendan called out the last name, Stewy turned to him in disappointment. Declan tried to keep a brave face but he could still feel his heart sinking. He knew everyone was a sub at some point but it still felt unfair. This could be their only match and there was a chance he wasn't going to play in it at all. He still felt happy Stewy was playing, though. It was great to see his best friend making the starting team.

Brendan then took a step forward. 'Lads, we've a great full-forward line,' he said. 'Let's get the ball up to them quickly and they'll do the damage. Every time Sligo have the ball, I want us tackling, putting them under pressure. We don't want them getting any easy scores.'

He then turned to the captain, Billy Graham.

'Billy, I was talking to a few of the other coaches before the game and they've a lad playing at centre-forward, Tadhg Conlon. He's meant to be a tricky player, so stick to him like glue.'

Billy nodded, a look of determination on his face.

'Alright, lads. Let's go out there and show them what we can do!'

'Come on, lads!' they all shouted.

As Declan walked towards the bench, he tried his best to keep his energy up, but he couldn't hide his frustration. He was bombarded with all sorts of thoughts. *Why wasn't I picked? Am I not good enough? If we lose, I won't even get a chance to play at all. My parents travelled all the way to see me – what if they came for nothing? I wanted to make them proud. I wanted to make my granddad proud. I wanted – Wait!* A lightbulb went on in his head. He suddenly remembered the magical word his grandfather had said to him: visualise.

He might not be able to play yet, but there was nothing stopping him from studying the rival team. It was better than sitting on the bench sulking. Of course, it was possible he could study the team for the entire match and still not be asked to join. But he'd kick himself if he was asked to play and hadn't prepared.

Away Days

Billy approached the middle of the pitch.
Declan could see the referee take a coin out
of his pocket as Billy shook hands with Sligo's
captain. Declan assumed he was the Conlon
guy Brendan had spoken about, as he was
wearing number 11, which meant he'd be
marking Billy. He wasn't that big but they had
been warned about him. A guy like that could
end their journey before it even began.

Conlon won the coin toss and indicated to
the referee he wanted to play with the wind.
As the players on both teams made their way
to their positions, Declan was determined to
keep a positive attitude and keep an eye on
Conlon. Even if Declan got on, he probably
wouldn't be too close to Conlon, as he'd be on
the opposite forward line, but he wanted to
be ready to make a contribution, as it seemed
Conlon was going to be their danger man.

The referee had a quick look at his watch,
then threw the ball in at the centre of the
pitch. Brian Bohan and their other midfielder,
Peter O'Sullivan, desperately tried to gain

possession. However, the big Sligo midfielder managed to catch the ball cleanly before taking off on a solo run.

'Look for Tadhg!' Declan heard the Sligo manager call out. Billy sprinted to try and tackle the Sligo midfielder but he hand-passed the ball over Billy's head, landing it into the grateful arms of Tadhg Conlon. Conlon took off like a rocket.

'Oh no,' Declan thought.

'Stop him! Tackle!' Brendan shouted frantically.

Conlon flew towards their goal, taking solos but not breaking stride at all. If anything, he seemed to be getting faster. Thankfully he curled the ball over the bar as their defence just about managed to clog up the space in front of him.

Declan breathed a sigh of relief. *I thought he was in for a goal there and the match isn't even a minute old!*

As the first half wore on, Stewy and Brian Bohan came into the game and played well.

However, Conlon was on fire. He always looked like he was going one way with the ball but would suddenly dart in the other direction as soon as any of the defenders got near him. He was a master of misdirection. It's hard to notice these things when you're on the field. Luckily, Declan could study Conlon and the other players from the bench. He zoned out for a few minutes and visualised what he would do if he was on the pitch. He pictured Conlon on the ball, trying to trick him. He always seemed to lean left before he went right. Declan visualised himself being ready for this and then taking the ball from Conlon as he darted to the right. Declan played that scene over in his mind a few times.

When the whistle blew for half-time, Sligo were up by two points. *OK. That's not too bad*, Declan thought. *We can recover from this*. He was on his way onto the pitch to warm up when Brendan called him. 'Declan. You're going on.' Declan's eyes lit up.

Benched

He walked over to the team, who were gulping down water. Brendan was standing in the middle with a tense look on his face.

'Lads, we're doing OK after a shaky start,' he said. 'We need more from everyone. There's not enough ball going in to David Jenkins. We need to win more breaks around midfield and we need to stop the ball going in to Tadhg Conlon. Cut off the supply. You know they're going to look for him every time, so try to dispossess them before they get it to him. Just one change, guys – Rory Bennett is coming off. Well done, Rory, good effort out there today. Declan Kirby is going on at wing-forward. Declan, you really impressed us in training and were very unlucky not to start. Go out there and try to make an impact. Let's go for it – we've nothing to lose! If we go home today, let's go home knowing that we've given every last bit of energy we have. Now, let's go and show them what we're about!'

As Declan jogged over to the wing-forward position, he knew this was the moment to put his grandfather's advice to the test. *Let's hope this visualisation technique pays off!* As soon as the second half began, his aim was to get on the ball as quickly as possible to settle himself down. Brian Bohan put a ball down the wing for him to chase. Declan outpaced the wing-back, then hand-passed it across to David Jenkins, who blasted it over the bar to bring it to a one-point game. As the game continued, it was hard to get on the ball as Sligo had so much possession.

With only five minutes left, Sligo were leading by two points. Conlon had been changed to midfield. He was making his way towards Declan with the ball. Since he was leaning to his left, Declan knew he was going to dart right. Just as he was approaching, Declan looked like he was going to lunge right but moved left at the last second. Sure enough, Conlon soloed the ball to his right, and Declan caught it with ease. He was so shocked Declan got the ball off him, he did a double-take. He was sure they had the game in the bag.

But now was not the time for Declan to get cocky. He didn't have much time and he only had one shot. As he sped towards the goal, two Sligo players made their way towards him. As they gained on him, he realised that he had to chance it. He took a breath and buried the ball to the back of the net.

The crowd of parents and supporters went wild. As Sligo desperately tried to move the ball down the pitch, Brian Bohan made a brilliant interception and laid it off to Paul Lynch, who raced forward and popped over a great point. It seemed to take an eternity, but minutes later, the ref blew the whistle. They'd beaten Sligo by three points, 1–14 to 1–11. As they made their way back to Brendan, Declan could feel his legs ache and beads of sweat dripping down his face. He was pretty tired, even though he'd only played half the game. He wondered how exhausted he would have been if he'd played the entire match.

Brendan started clapping to get their attention. 'Good job, guys. That was our first match together. We got off to a bad start but we came back really strong in the second half. Remember, this is only the beginning. You need to maintain that standard. Do yourselves proud.'

As soon as Declan walked out of the dressing room, his mum and dad ran over to him, their eyes bright with excitement.

'Well, looks like all those hours of practice paid off!' his dad said proudly.

'I was so upset when I didn't see you on the pitch,' his mum said. 'I thought you'd been hurt or you were ill or something. Then I saw you'd been benched – but after scoring that goal at the end, I bet they won't be doing that again!'

'They'd better not!' Declan said, laughing.

Benched

FINAL SCORE   1-14
1-11

Substitution: Declan Kirby (1–0) for Rory Bennett

Chapter 8

Winning

Paddy, the driver, pulled the bus up at a GAA centre just on the outskirts of Salthill. Salthill Knocknacarra GAA club had kindly offered the teams a meal after the match to show them true Galway hospitality. After David Jenkins had finished eating, he stood up and raised his cup.

'I'd like to make a toast,' he said jokingly. 'Yes, we were accepted into the county squad.'

'Hear, hear,' Big Mike said, raising his glass of water.

'And yes, we have won our first big match,' David continued.

'Thanks to Declan's last-minute goal!' Brian Bohan said, giving him a cheeky wink.

'Hey, lads!' Cathal Hayes interrupted. 'Don't forget about my point at the end!'

Suddenly, David's manner became very serious. 'But there is a more … pressing matter that we all forgot about. Something far more important. And that is … what's in Bushy's mystery box?'

'Oh yeah!' Brian Bohan shouted.

'I totally forgot about that!' said Big Mike.

'Come on, Bushers,' David said, egging him on. 'We left you alone on the bus. We didn't say a word in the dressing room. We've been pretty patient. You've kept us all in suspense. Spill the beans. What's inside it? Where is it?'

'It's in the last place you'll ever look,' Bushy mumbled. He kept his head down because he knew he would crack under the pressure if he made eye contact with David.

'Come on, Bushman,' David pleaded. 'You know you want to, Bushinator.'

'I'm not going to.'

'I'll give you two of my chips if you show it to me.'

'No.'

'Three chips.'

'Not going to happen.'

'One chip.'

'I'm not – wait, why would I show you the box for one chip if I just said no for three chips?'

'I don't know,' David said. 'I was trying to confuse you.'

'Well, it didn't work!' Bushy said victoriously.

'Righto.' David sighed as he walked towards the bathroom. 'I know when I'm beat. Can't change your mind. I'm just going to head to the toilet before we leave so –' David suddenly dived under the table, scrambling by Bushy's feet. 'I bet it's under here!'

'Knock it off, Jenkins,' Bushy barked.

As the pair got into a minor scuffle, the rest of the guys started cheering them on. Brian Bohan was just trying to start a Bushy chant when Brendan walked into the room.

'Knock it off, lads, or you can forget about being on the starting team tomorrow.'

David got to his feet and, as Brendan turned his back, looked at Bushy with a mischievous grin and whispered, 'Four chips. Final offer.'

'Keep dreaming, Jenkins,' Bushy replied.

'But seriously, I actually do have to go to the toilet,' David said and darted to the bathroom.

'Is your mysterious ... yoke OK?' Declan asked.

'Yeah, don't worry about it.'

'He didn't step on it, did he?'

'Nah, it's not here. I gave it to the bus driver for safe keep– eh ... I mean ...'

'Ah-ha!' Declan cried.

'Look, please don't tell Jenkins.'

'Oh no, I won't. I promise. I'm not even going to ask what's in it. You'll tell me when you feel the time is right.'

'Cheers. I appreciate that.'

'It's just ... I'm surprised you didn't ask me to keep it safe for you. Why did you ask the driver? You don't even know him!'

'It's fine. Paddy said his daughter is into the same stuff so he will be extra caref– oh, not again!' Bushy said, clasping his hands over his mouth.

'What?'

'You're being sneaky! You're trying to figure out what's inside it!'

'Well, it was worth a shot.'

As David passed by on his way back from the bathroom, Declan decided it would be best to change the subject. 'What do you think about all this anyway?'

'What do you mean?'

'Like, do you think we can win?'

'Well, we're obviously going to move on to the next round, right?' said Bushy.

'No, I mean, can we win ... the whole thing?'

'You really think we have a chance?' David said, leaning across the table.

'Would any of us be here if we thought we didn't?' Brian piped up.

'I'm surprised they made Billy captain,' Big Mike said. 'He's not tough enough. Where is he anyway?'

Winning

'He's over there,' Declan said, pointing in front of him.

'What's he eating?' Big Mike said, squinting in confusion.

'He told me his mum makes everything for him,' Declan explained. 'He has a weak stomach or something.'

'That's what I mean,' Big Mike said. 'Weak. We don't need weak. We need tough. If I was in charge, I'd crack down on everyone to make sure they're all giving 100 per cent. If we're not tough enough, we can't win.'

'Don't say that,' Brian snapped. 'You can't be dismissing our chances. All that negative talk doesn't help us. It just brings us down.'

'He's right.' Declan nodded. 'If even one player doubts that we can do this, that we can win every single match, then that doubt will seep in and affect how we play. We need to look at what's coming as if we're guaranteed to win.'

'Isn't that being a bit … full of ourselves?' Big Mike asked.

'No – it's being positive,' Declan said. 'If we think we can't get through this, we're not going to play our best. We need to act like victory is guaranteed. We still might lose, but at least we'll know we couldn't have tried harder.'

There was dead silence in the room. Brendan had been writing in his notepad, but now he was listening. All the guys were taking on board what Declan was saying. Then, because no one was speaking, he felt like he should break the awkward silence. 'Look, eh … I wasn't trying to make a big speech or anything. I just wanted to make sure we were all on the same page, y'know?'

'I've got it!' David shouted, jumping out of his seat.

'What?' Declan asked. 'What is it?'

David looked at Bushy and held out all the fingers on his left hand. 'Five chips! I'll give you five chips if you tell me what's in the box.'

'Oh, not this again!' Declan groaned.

Chapter 9

The Haunted Hotel

As the bus arrived at their hotel, Declan nudged Stewy, who was nodding off. 'We're here,' he said. 'Can't wait to see what my room is like.'

As they got to their feet, the bus jolted, causing David to bump into Paul Lynch. 'Hey, watch it!' Paul cried, pushing David back.

'You watch it!' David snapped with a violent shove.

'Oi!' Brendan shouted. 'I don't want any nonsense from anyone. Everyone is to be on their best behaviour. That's an order. If I have to deal with any trouble, not starting on the team will be the least of your worries. You'll be sent home.'

Declan had never heard Brendan speak with such authority – he usually had a gentle manner about him. But then again, who could blame him? He'd chosen each player for this squad because he believed they had a shot to win the competition. If they weren't taking it seriously and were messing around, it reflected badly on him.

David hung his head. 'Sorry, Brendan,' he mumbled.

'Won't happen again,' Paul said.

'It had better not,' Brendan said, staring at each of them in turn. 'All of you out. Now.'

As they got off the bus, they had their first proper look at the hotel.

'When was this built?' David asked. 'The Stone Age?'

'It's not that old,' Brian Bohan said.

'I know the budget isn't much but I thought

we'd stay in a hotel built in the last century or two!'

Although David was kidding, he did have a point. Declan hadn't expected the accommodation to be glamorous, but he was surprised Brendan couldn't find anywhere better.

Paul Lynch slowly leaned in to Declan and Stewy and whispered, 'What if it's haunted?'

They knew he was just trying to be funny, but it was hard not to think that way. They gazed at the crumbling, mossy building in cautious wonder.

Brendan quickly went in to announce the team's arrival at reception. Paddy began getting the cases out of the large compartment under the bus. He had plenty of volunteers to help, since nobody seemed to want to go into the hotel on their own.

Brendan came back out, with a perplexed look on his face. 'Come on, lads, we can't stay here all day! Let's get moving!'

As they stepped into the entrance area, a very old lady was waiting for them. Her hair

was chalk-white, contrasting with her full-black
suit. She wore thick glasses that sat on the
bridge of her nose.

'Hello, my name is Ms O'Gorman,' she said.
Although she sounded welcoming, her raspy
voice was a bit unnerving. She looked at the
boys in silence, as if she was trying to figure
out which ones were troublemakers. 'Now,' she
said in an unexpectedly strong voice. 'I must
tell you what rooms you are in. Most of them
are double rooms so you will be able to share
with a friend. Just one or two of them are
single rooms, but they are close to each other
so no one will feel scared being on their own.

'This is quite a large hotel, which means
that if you try exploring all the corridors and
staircases, you'll probably get lost. We don't
want that to happen, do we? I mean, the last
thing we would ever want is for you poor boys
to just ... disappear.'

Declan felt the hairs on the back of his neck
stand on end. Alarm bells were going off in his
head, roaring at him to get out of there.

'Each room has a number on the door,' she continued. 'I want lights out in the next half an hour and I don't want to hear another sound until half eight tomorrow morning.'

Ms O'Gorman suddenly moved behind the reception desk. For such an old woman, she could move quickly. 'Step forward in pairs,' she commanded. Despite her frail appearance, you'd swear she was a drill sergeant the way she ordered them around.

As they lined up, Bushy went to the very back. 'Hey, what are you doing?' Declan asked him.

'I just need to ask Ms O'Gorman something ... private.'

'Oh, OK,' Declan said, nodding. He and Stewy looked at each other – they both knew he was trying to secure one of the rooms on his own. Needless to say, if somebody stayed with him, they might uncover the contents of his secret box and he seemed determined to avoid doing that for as long as possible.

When Stewy and Declan got their keys, they made their way to their room. Declan was exhausted after the match. He unpacked quickly, leaving out his clothes for the morning, then brushed his teeth and jumped into bed.

'Last one standing turns off the light switch,' he said.

'Well, I've got a few more things to unpack so that'll be me then,' Stewy said. 'That Ms O'Gorman is so creepy looking.'

'Tell me about it,' Declan said, yawning. He wasn't in the mood for a long conversation, as he was struggling to keep his eyes open.

'With the white hair and the black suit, she looks like a ghost!' he said, his lip quivering slightly.

'Or a penguin!' Declan said, laughing, trying to calm him down.

It was clear the lads had done a good job of spooking Stewy. He kept looking around at the slightest noise. 'You don't think this place is haunted, do you?'

'The guys were just joking, Stewy,' Declan reassured him. 'Anyway, I'm shattered. I'm going to sleep.'

It didn't take long for Declan to nod off. But he was soon woken up by something whacking him in the chest. He opened his eyes and made out Stewy sitting straight up in bed.

'What are you doing?!' he said, half asleep.

'Declan!' he whispered. 'There's a noise!'

He could barely see Stewy in the dark but he could hear him trying to control his breathing. Whatever he'd heard had got him into a proper panic. 'It's an old hotel, Stewy,' Declan said, rubbing his eyes. 'There's going to be creaky noises. It's just your imagination running wild. We need our energy. We have a game tomorr–'

A high-pitched wailing sound interrupted him. It came from right outside their room. Declan had never heard anything like it in his life. The two of them just lay there, frozen stiff, waiting to hear if the noise would happen again.

After what felt like an eternity, they heard another noise. But this wasn't a wail. It was a scratching sound. Stewy grabbed Declan and clutched his arms tightly. 'It's scraping against our door!' he yelled.

Chapter 10

The Ghost in the Corridor

'Ow!'

'Dec! You OK?'

'You're digging into my arm!' he whispered, trying to control his volume. He didn't know why he was trying to stay quiet, though. Whatever was outside knew they were in there.

'W-what do you think it is?' Stewy said as quietly as he could.

'I don't know, but it's trying to find its way inside.'

The scraping started to get faster and louder as if this thing's life depended on it.

'It's a g-ghost,' Stewy stuttered.

'No way. It can't be. We haven't even seen what's out there.'

'I'm not chancing it,' Stewy squealed. With that, he leapt out of his bed and ducked under it. Declan was about to ask him to come out and stop acting silly, but he didn't like the idea of being in his bed by himself so he squeezed under Stewy's as well.

'What'll we do if it comes in?' Stewy whispered.

'I don't know,' Declan said honestly. 'How do you attack a ghost?'

'You can't hit it. If you throw something, it'll just pass through it. Ghosts can't touch things.'

'Wait ... how is it touching the door then?'

'I didn't read the manual on ghost rules, did I?' Stewy whispered with a hopeless look on his face. 'We can't fight it. We're going to have to beg for mercy to survive.'

Declan's eyes darted around the room, searching for a way out. He looked towards the window, but they were on the fourth storey and he didn't fancy the drop. He looked to the en suite. 'We could lock ourselves in the bathroom?' he said.

'Good idea,' Stewy said. 'But ... em ... you go first.'

'What? Why?'

'Because it's your plan.'

'Is that the rules?'

'Also, I warned you there was a ghost and you didn't believe me. So, if anyone is going –'

'Wait!' Declan said, still trying to keep his voice low. 'Listen.'

'What? I don't hear anything.'

'Exactly! The scraping. It's stopped.'

'OK, cool ... You check if it's gone.'

Declan just wanted this night to be over and done with, so he wasn't going to argue. 'Fine,' he sighed as he slowly crawled from underneath the bed.

The noise had definitely stopped. He looked around every part of the room to make sure there was nothing out of the ordinary.

'OK. The coast is clear,' he said to Stewy as he got to his feet. 'Turn on the light.'

'No way,' Stewy said, shaking his head. 'I'm not going near that door.'

As Stewy crawled out, they both heard a noise. It was a different sound but it was much scarier. They looked to the door to see the creaky door handle turning. Stewy opened his mouth to scream but no sound came out. As the door slowly opened, every fibre of Declan's being was telling him to get out of there. Get back under the bed. Hide in the bathroom. Break through the window. But he was so scared, he couldn't move a muscle.

As the door opened, in glided a small thin figure draped in white. It was hunched and wearing a veil on its head, so it was impossible for them to get a good look at its face. As the figure came closer, they took a step back. Declan's legs were quivering so much, he could barely stand.

The creature raised its head and made an inhumane squeal.

'Spare us,' Stewy pleaded as he fell to his knees. 'Please spare us, spirit. We'll do anything you want.'

The spectre raised its hands inches away from Declan's face. 'I am the ghost of Grangehill Castle,' it uttered in a hoarse voice.

'W-what do you want with us?' Stewy stammered.

'You have offended me. You must now pay the penalty.'

'W-what?' Stewy blubbered.

'I will haunt you. Haunt you ... forever.'

Declan had still been half asleep when the 'ghost' came in and hadn't been thinking straight, especially with Stewy in a state of panic. But he was becoming calm now. And the calmer he felt, the more suspicious he became of the new visitor.

'So where have you come from, Ghost of Grangehill Castle, or whatever you call yourself?' he said in a firm voice.

The ghost hesitated before pointing up towards the ceiling. 'From the ... um ... secret room,' it explained.

The Ghost in the Corridor

'From the "um" secret room?' Declan repeated. 'What ghost says "um"?'

He dived at the ghost and tackled it to the ground. As it wrestled with him, he pulled off its face-cover.

'Jenkins!' he exclaimed. 'I knew it was you by the way you said the word "penalty". You're always calling for a penalty if you're fouled anywhere near the square.'

'Get off me, Declan,' David Jenkins barked. 'You're hurting my arm. I won't be able to play in the next match.'

'You should have thought of that when you decided to act like an idiot!'

Suddenly, Paul Lynch jumped into the room, laughing his head off. 'Oh, man. You guys sounded scared stiff. I wish I could have seen your faces.'

'Was it really you making that noise out there?' Stewy said. It seemed he still hadn't got over his worst fears.

'Of course it was. What age are you? I stopped believing ghost stories when I was six!'

Their discussion was interrupted by a sound in the corridor. At first, Declan assumed it was one of the other lads who was in on the gag. But then he saw the confusion and concern on David and Paul's faces. They were just as clueless as him and Stewy.

'Is that Brendan?' Declan whispered to David.

'He's asleep,' David said, getting to his feet.

Whatever the sound was, it was getting louder, which could mean only one thing: it was coming closer.

Chapter 11

In Trouble

They all moved a step back. David Jenkins's face had gone whiter than the sheet he was wearing. Whatever it was, they could hear it coming up the stairs. Every time he heard a step creak, Declan tensed up. Stewy was in an utter panic. He'd just calmed down a moment before but managed to work himself into a frenzy all over again. Suddenly, the door burst open to reveal a horrid but familiar figure.

'Ms O'Gorman,' Declan cried.

'I thought as much,' she said with a raspy sigh. 'Delinquents. I knew I couldn't trust a group of footballers in this hotel.'

Her words cut through them like a knife. At that moment, Declan would have preferred it to have been a ghost rather than Ms O'Gorman.

'You!' she hissed, as she extended a bony finger towards David Jenkins. 'What are you doing covering yourself with one of this hotel's good bedsheets? Getting it filthy with one of your silly games?'

'S-sorry, Ms O'Gorman,' he mumbled, lowering his head.

'Sorry?' she repeated sarcastically. 'Sorry isn't good enough! And I suppose it was you making that awful noise that could be heard all over the hotel, waking everybody up?'

Nobody said anything. Paul Lynch slowly raised his hand. 'Em ... it was me who made the noises. Sorry, ma'am.'

'Ms O'Gorman,' she screeched. 'You can address me as Ms O'Gorman.'

In Trouble

'Sorry, Ms O'Gorman.'

'What are your names?

'Paul Lynch and David Jenkins.'

'Don't think your coach won't be hearing about this first thing in the morning,' she said, shaking her finger at them. 'If it was up to me, I'd send you home in a heartbeat.'

Declan could see the boys' hearts sinking just with the idea that they might not play on the team again.

Ms O'Gorman suddenly interrupted their thoughts. 'GET TO YOUR ROOMS IMMEDIATELY!' she roared.

As they darted out, she continued to call after them. 'And if I hear one more sound from either of you, I'll be recommending to your coach that you are sent back home altogether and that'll be the end of your trip.'

She then turned to Stewy and Declan. Declan wanted to defend himself and his best friend, saying none of this was their idea. However, he felt like Ms O'Gorman was in such a rage that anything he said would fall on deaf ears.

'You two,' she said. 'Get back to bed and don't open that door to anyone. We've had enough silliness tonight to last a lifetime.'

'Yes, Ms O'Gorman,' they said together and got back into their beds immediately, before she slammed the door.

As Declan was trying to take in everything that had just happened, Stewy piped up. 'Dec, what do you think Brendan is going to do when he hears about this?'

'I don't know,' he said honestly. 'But we need those guys on the team. If Brendan sends them home, we don't stand a chance.'

Chapter 12

Consequences

At breakfast, the boys had plenty to talk about following the previous night's antics. Nobody wanted to get in any more trouble, so all the chatting was done in whispers while they tried to avoid Ms O'Gorman's eyes. They didn't dare laugh aloud and some of them kept looking over their shoulder to make sure Ms O'Gorman wasn't nearby.

The smiles and smirks were wiped off everybody's faces as Brendan walked in.

Unknown to them, Ms O'Gorman had already spoken to him in private and informed him of the night's capers. He stared at them all in silent anger before beckoning Paul Lynch and David Jenkins towards the reception area. The pair sheepishly plodded over. As they walked past, Declan could see the terror in their eyes – you'd swear they were in the presence of a tiger. He wondered what was going to happen. Was this to be the end of their trip?

'Right, boys,' Brendan started. 'What was the first thing I said before you got off the bus yesterday?'

'Be on our best behaviour,' David answered immediately.

'And you two let me down on the first night. THE FIRST NIGHT!' he shouted. 'I am shocked you two are so irresponsible. I thought you were sensible, the types who'd set a good example. You don't have an ounce of common sense, do you? DO YOU?'

Paul looked confused. 'No, sir. I mean, I do, sir. I mean – I do ... but I didn't last night ... sir.'

'As I said to you before,' Brendan continued, 'you are representing not only yourselves here but your county. If anything like this happens again with you two, both of you will be sent home. But for now, the pair of you are dropped for the Westmeath match.'

'W-what?' Paul stuttered.

'You won't be playing one minute of the next match,' Brendan said, frowning. 'Now get out of my sight.'

As Brendan turned to walk away, David called out to him. 'Wait, Brendan. We're really sorry. Genuinely.'

'You know nothing like this will ever happen again,' Paul promised. 'I mean ... what we did ... it's not on. But when we're in the match, there's no messing about. You know we'll give 100 per cent. We always do.'

'Please,' David said. 'I love playing on this team. It means so much to me. I'm sorry about last night. It was just a laugh, and I shouldn't have done it.'

Brendan had a sadness in his eyes. He hated upsetting the kids but he had to be strict or the whole team could fall apart. 'Look, lads, I appreciate the apologies and it shows good character that you can admit when you're in the wrong. But you still won't be playing in the Westmeath game. If we can get over that match and you two stay out of trouble, you should be alright.'

David and Paul were devastated. You could see by their faces that they'd accepted defeat. They knew pushing the issue would only make it worse. Without saying a word, they headed back to the table and continued eating their cereal. Stewy and Declan just looked at each other awkwardly. Declan wanted to say something to make them feel better but he wasn't sure how they'd take it.

It was worrying that they weren't playing. David and Paul were among the best players, and the team would suffer out there without them. But if Brendan made an exception for them, other players might start messing around. It was annoying but Declan understood why Brendan had to give such a harsh punishment.

But it got worse: Declan now had a new objective. Not only did they have to win the game, he had to make sure Paul and David stayed out of trouble for the rest of the trip. He honestly couldn't say which was going to be harder to achieve.

Chapter 13

Making the Team

As they geared up for the match against Westmeath, Brendan called out who was playing. By that point, everyone was aware of Paul and David's prank the night before. The team knew Brendan had punished them both so no one was surprised when their names weren't called out. Some of the team members complained about it later on the bus, saying Brendan had been too harsh.

Declan thought there was no point whining about it – there was nothing they could do to change it. Since breakfast, he'd been thinking how they could adjust their tactics without David or Paul. Not having either of them on the team was going to hurt their chances of winning this game.

Just before they headed onto the pitch, Brendan told them, 'Westmeath are well-organised. They'll be tough. You must be patient. Stick to what I've told you to do and we'll give them a few problems.'

As soon as the game started, Declan saw Brendan wasn't exaggerating. Westmeath were like a well-oiled machine. They got an early lead, scoring a point within a matter of seconds. Minutes later, they put the ball over the bar for the second time.

After playing for only a few moments, Declan could feel the doubt setting in. No matter how hard he tried or how fast he ran, he couldn't get near the ball. Ten minutes in and he already felt winded.

Could this be it? he thought. *Is this our last game? Would David and Paul playing have made the difference between us winning and losing? Did Brendan make a mistake when he said they couldn't play? Should I have said something to stick up for them?*

He was suddenly shaken from his thoughts by a loud cheer from the crowd. He looked up to see Brian Bohan had scored a point. *Thank goodness*, he thought. He needed something positive to shake off the negativity swelling up inside him. Being in a negative mood was no good to anyone.

Peter O'Sullivan then blasted the ball over the bar, levelling the score. 'Yes!' Declan cried. They'd had a rough patch in the beginning, but they still had a chance. They could still win without Paul and David. Harry and Dereck hadn't been able to play for this team and they'd still won their last match – maybe they could win any game if they were determined enough.

Just before half-time, the scores were level at five points apiece. Then Jack Maher sent Declan in a lovely ball that landed right onto his chest. He sidestepped the corner-back to leave just the keeper in front of him. He tried to round him but the keeper took him down. He heard the referee's whistle and saw him holding his arms out to indicate a penalty. With neither Paul nor David on the pitch, no one had been designated penalty-taker, so Declan got the ball and placed it on the spot.

He knew he had to make his decision and stick with it. He was going to hit it low and hard to the left, as near to the post as possible. He took the run-up and struck it well – low into the bottom corner for a goal! *Yes!* Now it was 1–5 to 5 points.

Nothing boosts your confidence more than scoring a goal. As Declan jogged back to his wing-forward position, he felt a surge of energy going through his body – he wanted to get the ball as much as possible. As the goalkeeper kicked out the ball, the referee blew for half-time.

As the boys downed water, Brendan began to talk. 'Lads, we've grown into this game and

we've really only started to play in the last
ten minutes. Let's keep that momentum at
the start of the second half.' Then he looked
at Declan. 'Great penalty, Declan. We really
needed that. Lads, we haven't played well
but we're in the lead. *I* know what great
footballers you are, but I want you to show
everybody watching this game how good you
are. Remember, work hard for each other, take
your scores when they come and be totally
disciplined. No giving away silly frees. Now, go
out and let's do this!'

The referee threw the ball up at the start
of the second half and Brian Bohan made a
clean catch. He immediately raced towards the
Westmeath goal. *He's like a train when he gets
going*, Declan thought as he tried to keep up.
The big Westmeath full-back ran out to tackle
him but he quickly laid the ball off to Declan.

Bang!

The ball smacked off the top of the crossbar
and went over for a point.

'Ohhh! Close one, Declan!' Brendan
shouted. 'But that's great play, lads, keep it up!'

Making the Team

The Westmeath keeper took the kick-out
but it was caught by Peter O'Sullivan, who then
spotted Stewy running forward. O'Sullivan hit
a crisp kick pass into Stewy's chest, who then
curled the ball over the bar. They were really in
the zone now, Declan thought. But then ...

'Arrrgh!' their centre-back, Billy Graham,
yelled, holding his stomach.

'Billy! What's wrong?' Brendan shouted from
the sideline.

Declan turned around to see Billy slumped
on the ground.

'My stomach!' Billy said, looking deathly
pale. 'It doesn't feel right. I can't get up.' He
was white as a ghost.

'OK,' Brendan said, with a worried look on
his face.

Declan could see Paul and David giving him
the puppy eyes, hoping he would let them play,
but he was having none of it.

He turned to Robert Casey. 'Robert, you're
going on.'

Robert was a decent player, but Billy was
an excellent centre-back, and they began to

feel his loss immediately, with Westmeath playing with more urgency. Their midfielders came more into the game and began powering forward at every opportunity. With five minutes remaining, Westmeath had clawed their way back to within two points and the ball broke out to Big Mike.

'Mike!' Declan shouted.

Big Mike kicked a cross-field ball towards Declan, who ran on to it at pace. He gathered it, then began to run.

'Go, Declan!' Brendan shouted from the sideline.

He sidestepped the centre-back coming out towards him. Then, as the full-back came charging in Declan's direction, he hand-passed out to Peter O'Sullivan, who lofted a high ball in towards the goal mouth.

It hung in the air for what seemed like minutes.

Then it dawned on Declan. *It's going over.*

The ball just crept over the bar to put them three points up.

A few minutes later, with their backs frantically defending, the referee blew the final whistle.

'Yes!' Declan shouted as he fell to his knees, exhausted.

He then felt a tap on his shoulder. It was the Westmeath wing-back.

'Hey, great game, man. Best of luck in the next one,' he said as he held out his hand.

'Thanks,' Declan breathlessly managed to get out.

In the end, it seemed that Declan's goal had made all the difference, since they won 1–10 to 10 points. He'd only got one point in the second half, but it didn't matter. The goal he'd scored at the end of the first half had proved significant.

As the team all started high-fiving each other, David and Paul ran onto the pitch to congratulate Declan.

'Looks like you didn't need us after all,' David said. It was obvious he was gutted he didn't get a chance to play, but he didn't blame Declan for that. He knew he'd screwed up and he was just glad the rest of the team hadn't suffered without him.

'Way to go, man,' Paul said with a reassuring nudge. 'You know you're the only player to score a goal in both games?'

'Cheers,' Declan said modestly. 'I just thought of some of the little tricks you guys use when you play and tried my best to do them myself.'

'Tricks?' David said, dumbfounded. 'Dude, I just kick the ball! That's how far my strategy goes.'

'Attention, please!' Brendan shouted as he jogged towards them waving his hand. 'Couple of things I need to say. First off, well done. Solid game for you all. Keep that up because your next match is tomorrow morning. I just got off the phone and learned you'll be playing Roscommon.'

Despite their victory, he didn't seem too pleased. Something else was clearly on his mind. After an awkward silence, Stewy piped up. 'Is something wrong, Brendan?'

'Yes.' He sighed. 'As you know, your captain, Billy, was taken off.'

'Yeah, is he OK?' Paul enquired.

'He's got food-poisoning. The lunch he'd brought from home was off.'

A gasp could be heard all around. Stewy and Declan looked at each other in disbelief. They were so chuffed with winning the match, they hadn't even noticed Billy wasn't with them.

'You know what that means,' Brendan said ominously. 'We need a new captain. Now.'

Paul stuck his hand in the air and started waving it around like crazy.

'Not a chance, Paul,' Brendan said.

'Worth a shot,' he muttered.

As David raised his hand, Brendan gave a deep sigh. 'If I shot down Paul, what chance do you have, David?'

'I don't want to be captain,' he said. 'I think it should be Declan.'

'What?' Declan yelled. It caught him so off-guard, he wasn't sure what to say.

'How about it, Declan?' Brendan asked. 'Are you up to it?'

This was crazy. They'd just won the match five minutes ago and suddenly he was being pushed into being the leader of the team. It was all too much. He felt like he couldn't agree without checking if anyone else was interested. 'What about Big Mike? He always said he wanted to be the leader.'

'You're right,' Mike said. 'I want to be the captain ... but you *need* to be captain. What I want to do works for me. What you want to do will work for everybody.'

As Declan looked around to see if anyone else was stepping up for the position, he was met with silence. All he could see was a lot of encouraging faces. How could he say no?

'Yeah,' he said to Brendan. 'Captain it is.'

Making the Team

FINAL SCORE

1-10
0-10

Substitution: Robert Casey for Billy Graham

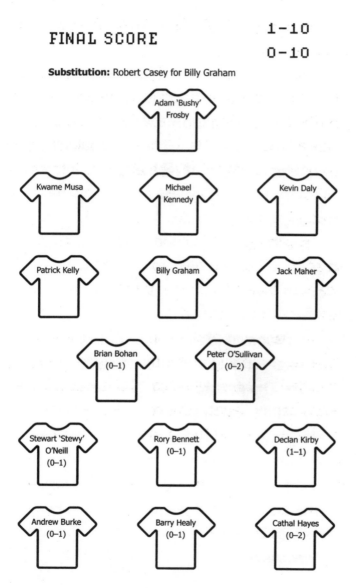

Adam 'Bushy' Frosby

Kwame Musa

Michael Kennedy

Kevin Daly

Patrick Kelly

Billy Graham

Jack Maher

Brian Bohan (0–1)

Peter O'Sullivan (0–2)

Stewart 'Stewy' O'Neill (0–1)

Rory Bennett (0–1)

Declan Kirby (1–1)

Andrew Burke (0–1)

Barry Healy (0–1)

Cathal Hayes (0–2)

Chapter 14

In Charge

Declan struggled to sleep after Brendan made him captain. It was a lot of responsibility to shoulder. The next morning, he quickly downed his breakfast and then rang his mum. He'd wanted to ring her the night before, but he felt like he needed some time to think. He hoped listening to her voice would soothe his nerves.

The phone rang three times before she picked up. 'Hello?'

'Hey, it's me.'

'Oh, lovely to hear from you, Declan. I hope you're all playing well.'

'Yeah.' He sighed.

'You're staying out of trouble?'

'Yep.'

'And Brendan is happy with you?' she asked.

'Well, that's the reason I wanted to speak to you.'

'Oh no,' she gasped. 'What's wrong? What did you do?'

'No, it's not like that. Brendan's made me captain of the team.'

'Oh my goodness!' she said. 'That's amazing! Here I am praying that you'll win every match but now they've made you captain – that's big news! You must be doing something right.'

'Mm-hm,' Declan grunted.

'Well, you don't sound too excited,' she said, disappointed. 'You sound like you've been sent home. You should be happier than anyone on that team!'

'Sorry, Mum. It's just ... it all happened so fast. The captain got sick yesterday, so they gave me the position, and we're playing a match today. If we lose, we're not just going home. People will notice that we lost the second I was made captain. They'll blame me. They'll say it's my fault.'

'Brendan wouldn't have given you the position if he thought you'd let everyone down, sweetie,' she reassured him. 'If you lose, it won't be because of you. It'll be in spite of you. I've never known you to give less than 100 per cent. You can only do your best.'

And just like that, he felt like a huge weight lifted off his chest. His mum always supported his love for the sport. She knew exactly what to say to make him feel better.

'Thanks, Mum. I really mean it.'

'Dad's gone to work, but Granddad's here. And – wait, hold on.' Mum's voice sounded muffled, as if she was speaking to someone in the background. 'Sorry, that was your grandfather. He just shouted "Jesse Owens!" Does that mean anything to you?'

'Yeah,' Declan said with a smile. 'It does.' As he looked up, he noticed Stewy waving at him and then pointing outside. 'Eh, Mum, the bus pulled up. I've got to go.'

* * *

Before the match, Brendan had a few things to say. 'Lads, this is the quarter-final, so of course Roscommon are a great team and are going to be tough to beat. I managed to catch the second half of their game against Longford. They have an excellent goalkeeper – he must have saved three or four one-on-ones during the time I was there. So, lads, only go for a goal if it's clearly on – otherwise, put the ball over the bar. A point might not seem like much, but if we keep the scoreboard ticking over throughout the game, it could be the difference between winning and losing.'

As Declan walked towards the centre of the pitch for the coin toss, he felt proud. Only a few days ago, he wasn't starting: now he was the captain. Declan won the coin toss and opted to play with the slight breeze.

When the match began, it seemed clear that there wasn't going to be much between the teams. For the first time since the beginning of the competition, they got on the scoreboard first, after Brian Bohan played a diagonal ball in to David Jenkins, who turned to curl over a lovely point with his right foot after about two minutes.

But Roscommon weren't going to make it easy for them. It was the most even game they had played. Every time they scored, Roscommon equalised within minutes. They were efficient, disciplined and methodical. Declan's team couldn't wait for them to make mistakes – they weren't making any.

The tactic of not trying to force goal opportunities seemed to be working, as Declan's team took their chances for points where they created them. When the half-time whistle blew, each team had five points. Declan hadn't scored yet, but that didn't matter for now. Winning was what was important.

As soon as the second half began, it was like Roscommon were playing at double speed. Whatever pep-talk they'd got at half-time seemed to have cranked their skills up a notch. Declan shouldered their centre-back as he was coming out with the ball and it was like his body was made of iron. He wasn't going to give an inch, and neither were the rest of his team.

Declan's team worked harder than they ever had, matching point for point throughout. As the second half neared to a close, the score was 0–10 to 0–9, and with the final whistle looming, it looked like they were going to lose by a single point.

As David got the ball, Declan saw him hesitate for a second. He glanced quickly towards Brendan on the sideline and then made a dash for the goal. He wasn't going for a point. He was trying for a goal. Declan knew he should have been annoyed David wasn't sticking with the plan, but a goal this late in the game would guarantee victory.

The Roscommon players were getting desperate, and two of them lunged at David. Although the first one missed him, the second one committed a foul. The ref blew the whistle for a free kick. They could easily get a point, but that would lead to a draw. Declan wasn't sure what to do. Should they risk it and try to win during extra time?

As he was thinking to himself, David ran up to him. 'This one could decide it, Dec. Who should take the shot?' Declan didn't expect him to ask, but as captain, he felt he had to make a decision. Although Declan had scored goals in the last two games, he felt like he hadn't played his best in this game, so he didn't think he should take the free kick himself. He knew Paul was great at frees and penalties, but he decided to try something else.

'You do it,' Declan said confidently.

'M-me?' David spluttered. 'Paul is a way better shot than me.'

'But you're stronger. Their goalkeeper is too good. If Paul or I took the shot, he'd probably catch it. But you kick with a lot of force. If you hit hard enough, he won't be able to hold on to it. Trust me.'

And with that, David went back and got the ball into his hands. Declan could see him concentrating and taking a deep breath. The pressure was getting to him, but he tried his best to keep his cool. He suddenly blasted the ball right at the goalkeeper. Although the keeper stopped it, he couldn't hold on to it and it dropped in front of him. As he ran to pick it up, Paul came out of nowhere and walloped it to the top-right corner of the net.

GOAL! That was it! They'd done it. Less than a minute later, the ref blew the final whistle. They were officially in the semi-final. As they all cheered and jumped around, Declan could see Brendan raising his fists in the air in triumph. He had never seen Brendan get emotional before, but he was clearly proud of his team.

As Declan went around to pat everyone on the back, Paul ran up to him, holding up his hand for a high five. 'Wow! Dec, well done! I was sure we were going for extra time.'

'No, well done to *you*, Paul – you were the one who got the goal.'

'Ah, who cares, man – we're in the semi-final! Wahoo!'

Away Days

FINAL SCORE

1-9
0-10

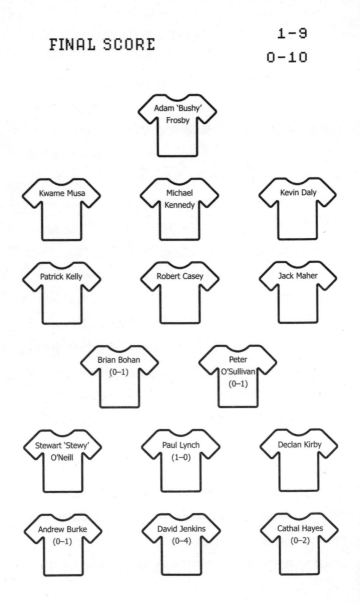

Adam 'Bushy' Frosby

Kwame Musa · Michael Kennedy · Kevin Daly

Patrick Kelly · Robert Casey · Jack Maher

Brian Bohan (0–1) · Peter O'Sullivan (0–1)

Stewart 'Stewy' O'Neill · Paul Lynch (1–0) · Declan Kirby

Andrew Burke (0–1) · David Jenkins (0–4) · Cathal Hayes (0–2)

Chapter 15

Train Station

'You know what would be cool, Declan?' Stewy asked as he lay on his bed the following morning. 'Going on a summer holiday.'

'Mm-hm,' Declan grunted, half-listening while he read his football magazine.

'I want to go to Poland. I mean, I always wanted to but it would be cool because a few of the lads could go and we could see Harry, y'know? Like, surprise him. I bet he'd appreciate that.'

'Mm-hm.'

'I'm an alien called Zarbodox.'

'Mm-hm.'

'You're not even listening to me!' Stewy shouted, throwing a shoe at Declan. 'Whoa, sorry,' he said, ducking a little too late.

'We're in the semi-final, Dec,' he said. 'You should be buzzin'. You're the captain so you should be happier than anyone, but you've had that same glum face since yesterday. You look gloomier than the bloody team we beat!'

'It's hard to explain, Stew. I feel like I let you guys down.'

Stewy was clearly taken aback. 'But … we won. Two more victories and we'll be champions of the country!'

'I know,' Declan said, forcing a smile.

'So why are you down?'

'I didn't even score!' he said, any trace of a smile disappearing. 'I scored in the first two matches. Brendan thought I had potential and so he made me captain. And I didn't score a goal. I didn't even get a single point. He'll probably take the captaincy off me the second Billy recovers.'

'Declan, you're looking at this totally wrong. You don't need to score to be a good player. You set us up with plenty of chances. You never hog the ball. If you think another player has a better chance of scoring, you give it to them. You could have taken that free yesterday but you trusted your gut and gave it to David. And because you decided to do that, you are the reason we won.'

Stewy and Declan always had a good laugh, but it was at times like this he realised why they were best friends. Some of the other players might tease him for talking like this. But Stewy didn't. He always put his mind at ease.

Most of the others had gone to Salthill again, like they did most days, but Declan and Stewy were too tired to join them this time. They had a one-day break to recover before the semi-final.

'I don't know what I'd do without you, Stewy. You're right. I'm looking at this whole thing in a way that's not helpful.'

'It's good to be tough on yourself sometimes. If you thought you were great all the time, you wouldn't get better. But you're not going to get better either if you put yourself down when you've done a lot of good.'

Knock, knock.

'What's that?' Declan asked.

'This better not be another one of David's stupid pranks,' Stewy said in a huff as he stormed towards the door. 'Because if it is, there'll be war!'

He opened the door to reveal Bushy in a sweat with his mysterious box tucked under his arm. 'Declan!' he shrieked. 'I need you. Now!'

'Calm down, man,' he said, holding his arms out. 'What's up?'

'Do you have Google Maps on your phone?'

'Eh ... yes. Why?'

'No time to explain!' he said in a frenzy. 'I need you to follow me. You too, Stewy!'

'What?' Stewy mumbled, confused.

Before they had a chance to agree to anything, Bushy legged it down the corridor.

'*Bushy!*' Declan yelled, trying to keep up. 'Where are we going? You know we're not allowed to leave the hotel.'

'It's OK, Declan,' he reassured him, still marching forward. 'I got special permission from Brendan and from my parents. They said I'm allowed to go if I bring two people with me.'

'What are we doing? You haven't told us anything! Where are we going?'

'The train station,' he yelled back.

'The train station? Why?'

'Lost track of time, Dec,' Bushy said, keeping up his swift pace. 'Was too busy preparing. Forgot to charge my phone and now my battery is dead.'

'Preparing for what?' Stewy shouted.

'You'll see,' he said cryptically.

Chapter 16

Wilbur

As Bushy, Stewy and Declan arrived on the platform, Declan took a moment to catch his breath. *I shouldn't be running like this*, he thought. *I'm supposed to be saving my strength for the game tomorrow.*

Bushy was looking around frantically. 'Quick. What time is it?'

'The clock there says it's 2 p.m. I think it's time you told us what this is all about,' said Declan, panting.

'I know,' Stewy said seriously.

'Y-you do?' said Bushy.

'I've known for a while.' Stewy nodded, smiling. 'Bushy is an undercover FBI agent based in Ireland.' He gave Bushy a curious look. 'Eh ... your name is Bushy, right?'

After a moment, Bushy slowly held up his mysterious box and, for the first time, popped the lid. Declan gasped, realising this was the first time he would see what was inside. As Bushy lifted back the lid, Declan waited for him to pull out the contents. Instead, he just stared into the box.

'Come on, don't be shy,' he whispered, giving the box a little shake. Suddenly, a little white face poked out and stared at them with its beady eyes.

'It's a rabbit!' Stewy said, with sheer joy in his voice.

'His name is Wilbur,' Bushy said. 'You can touch him, but be gentle. He's shy around strangers.'

As Declan took a step closer, he could see Wilbur was happily bedded down on straw, nibbling away at fresh carrots. Bushy had always loved animals. He had two dogs, one cat and a goldfish. He'd had rabbits in the past but Dec hadn't seen this one before. Bushy must've bought him recently.

'He's the best rabbit I've ever owned,' Bushy said proudly. 'Wilbur will be a champion.'

'A champion?' Stewy said, looking puzzled. 'How is he going to be a champion? Is he going to be our new captain?'

'It's for a pet show,' Bushy explained. 'I got an e-mail from the organisers just before this tournament started. They told me to be there today no later than twenty past two to register. It starts at half two.'

All of a sudden, they heard the sound of a train approaching. As it pulled up, Bushy put the lid back on the box before stepping onto the train. He turned to Stewy and Declan. 'Come on. Your tickets are already paid for.'

'Bushy, where are we going?' Declan asked as they followed him.

'Galway city,' he replied with a frustrated sigh. They found a few seats and felt the train begin to move. 'I wish the show had been nearer to the hotel.'

'Why didn't you just leave earlier?' Stewy said. 'Then there would have been no need for this big rush.'

'I know, but this morning I was using this special rabbit shampoo I got last week, and I was combing and brushing Wilbur to have him looking great.'

Stewy burst out laughing and bent over so low, Declan thought he was going to fall over. 'There's rabbit shampoo?' he asked in hysterics. 'Now I've heard everything!'

'You're lucky you got that private room,' Declan said. 'Otherwise you wouldn't have been able to do any of that without nonstop interruption and hassle.'

'Tell me about it. Especially with David Jenkins knocking around.'

'It's unbelievable that the show was in Galway the same time as the tournament.'

'I knew there was only a tiny chance of getting Wilbur to the show. But even if we couldn't make it, at least we'd be spending time together. I've only had him a few months and I didn't want to leave him at home by himself. This way, I can keep an eye on him every day.'

As Declan felt the train start to slow down, Bushy nudged him. 'We need to find this place. Get Google Maps out. It's not far but I don't know exactly where it is.'

As they got off the train, Declan could see on the map that the building was less than a five-minute walk but it was in an awkward spot. They never would have found it if it wasn't for his phone. They didn't have long to get there, so they dashed off as quickly as they could with Wilbur's box tucked tightly under Bushy's arm.

They arrived at the building with literally a minute to spare. Bushy ran so fast that people were hopping out of his way, probably thinking something terrible must have happened. But nothing would be worse for Bushy than missing the deadline, especially after all the trouble he had gone to hiding Wilbur for the last few days.

After signing the registration form, Bushy was brought to his spot by an official. Although he was wrecked, Bushy didn't take a breather. He took Wilbur out and stroked him to make sure his fur was smooth. Wilbur suddenly started thumping his foot.

'Why's he doing that?' Declan asked.

'He's nervous,' Bushy said. 'His fur is a mess. Where's his comb?'

Stewy gawked at Declan with his jaw open and mouthed 'rabbit comb' in disbelief. He wanted to laugh but he knew he had to be supportive of Bushy.

Their conversation was interrupted by a loud bell.

'What's that?' Declan said.

'The contest has officially started,' Bushy explained. 'Wish me luck.'

Chapter 17

The Competition

One of the organisers came up to Bushy, Stewy and Declan with a bottle of water. 'Hi, boys. Would you like a –?' Before he had a chance to finish his sentence, Bushy grabbed the bottle, popped the lid and downed the whole thing in a matter of seconds. He was so thirsty, it was like he'd spent all day in the desert. Declan had never seen someone drink that fast.

When Bushy finished, the organiser looked at them in shock. 'Em ... that was for the rabbit.'

The Competition

They all just stared at each other awkwardly, not knowing what to say. 'Good luck,' he said. As he walked off, the judge came over.

He was an older gentleman with a white beard and glasses. As he approached, he smiled and shook Bushy's hand. 'Hello, there. My name is Hennessy. I hear that you have been a very committed young man, coming here in the middle of your football tournament.' He then looked down at the rabbit and smiled. 'And this little chap is Wilbur, I presume.'

'Th-thanks. I mean, yes,' Bushy said nervously.

The judge examined Wilbur very carefully. You could tell that this wasn't just a fun little project for him. This was his life. He checked the rabbit so carefully, it was clear he had done this many, many times.

'OK, interesting,' he said to himself while feeling Wilbur's ears. Bushy glanced at Declan in a panic. Hennessy didn't give anything away. They didn't know if he thought Wilbur was great or appalling. Every now and again, he would scribble something on his clipboard. Declan could see Stewy trying to read it but Hennessy kept the board tight to his chest.

After a few minutes, he backed away from them. 'Well, I think I've got everything I need. I still have a few more to see. Have a look around, boys.'

'Thank you,' Bushy muttered. He had taken his other pets to competitions so Declan assumed this was all second nature to him, but Declan had never seen him act this nervous. He was probably extra stressed because they had rushed to get there, and he was probably also thinking of the upcoming match.

While Hennessy looked at the other contestants, the three boys wandered around the building. There were rows and rows of cages with other rabbits, guinea pigs and hamsters. There were many rabbits, so it looked like Wilbur had a lot of competition.

Declan knew that Bushy was worried that all the running around had unsettled Wilbur, so he tried to get him to look at the cats, dogs and hamsters. If he looked at the other rabbits, he'd just psych himself out. After about an hour, they saw Hennessy walking up the steps of the stage.

'Can I have your attention, please!' he bellowed. 'Looking at the rabbits this year, it is clear many contestants have upped their game. It was very close but there can only be one winner.

'Third place goes to Patty O'Hara. Well done, Patricia. This is her first time partaking in a show – you should be proud of yourself for coming third.'

As the three boys applauded, a girl of about their age walked up to the podium with her black and white rabbit to collect her rosette and a box of sweets.

'In second place,' Hennessy continued, 'we have Philip Loughlan. Well done on the runner-up prize, Phil.'

As Philip collected his prize and rosette, Bushy looked at Declan and Stewy anxiously. He was so nervous, he looked like he was literally in pain. He'd made such an effort to get Wilbur there that it would crush him to walk away with nothing.

'And, ladies and gentlemen, the moment you have all been waiting for,' Hennessy announced. 'First place in this year's rabbit category goes to the one and only ... Adam Frosby!'

'Ah, come on!' Stewy shouted, frowning and stamping his foot.

'YES!' Bushy screamed with his hands raised to the ceiling.

'What are you so happy about?' Stewy asked.

'Stew, Adam Frosby is Bushy,' Declan explained.

'YOUR NAME IS FROSBY?' Stewy yelled.

'What's wrong with you? The coach says his name when he calls out the players every game!'

Stewy was deep in thought. 'I never listen to that part – I only listen out for my own name!'

Bushy wasn't even listening to Stewy's comments. He was hysterical with joy. He ran up to the podium, shook Hennessy's hand and took his trophy. Everyone could see how ecstatic Bushy was and the audience was clearly having a good laugh about it. Bushy was so happy, you'd think he won the All-Ireland final.

Hennessy also handed him an envelope and a small box. 'There's your €20 prize there, kid. Enjoy it. And you get sweets, chocolates and a few nibbly bits for Wilbur. And for the record … I always say it's close because it makes people feel better when they don't win. But between me and you, as soon as I saw your rabbit, I knew he was going to be the winner. You obviously take really good care of him.'

'Thank you,' Bushy said, trying to hold back tears. When he got back to Declan and Stewy, he gave Wilbur some treats before placing him back in the box. He then held his hands out in triumph. 'Aren't you going to congratulate me?'

Before Declan had a chance to say anything, Stewy blew a gasket. 'WHAT KIND OF NAME IS FROSBY?'

Chapter 18

Tyrone

When Bushy, Stewy and Declan got back, it seemed Brendan had let the cat out of the bag and told the other guys where they had gone. Declan could see them in the lobby of the hotel giggling to themselves as the boys walked in. David locked eyes with Bushy and strode up to them with a gleeful smile from ear-to-ear.

'He's gonna try to wind you up, Bush,' Declan said. 'Don't take it to heart.'

'I don't care what he says,' Bushy replied. 'I won. Wilbur is a champion.'

As David stood in front of them, Declan expected him to start poking fun at Bushy or trying to grab the rabbit. Instead, David just politely said, 'Can I please see your bunny?'

'Wh-what?' Bushy stammered. This was the first time David had spoken to him without making fun of him.

'Why didn't you tell me you had a rabbit?' David said, sounding genuinely hurt. 'Rabbits are literally my favourite animal. My first pet, Buttons, was a little white rabbit.'

'So is he,' Bushy said as he popped the lid off the box. Wilbur poked his head out and started sniffing the air.

'He looks just like him!' David said excitedly, as he automatically went to pick him up.

'Hey!' Bushy yelled. 'Don't drop him!'

'I would never hurt him,' David said, keeping eye contact with the rabbit. 'He's an angel.'

By this point, all the other boys had run up to check out little Wilbur. Big Mike gave them a wave. 'Hey, lads. How did you get on at the –?' Big Mike stopped talking as soon as he saw Bushy's trophy. 'Oh my god! You won?'

'Of course he did!' David snapped. It was strange hearing David defending Bushy so passionately. 'How could he lose with this little guy? Best rabbit I ever saw ... apart from Buttons.'

The lads had been excited at the chance to see a rabbit, but now they were even more enthusiastic because Bushy had actually won. They bombarded him with so many questions that it was impossible to answer them all.

'Where's a good pet store to buy one?'

'What do you feed it?'

'Can dogs enter?'

'How often are these pet shows?'

'How do you prepare them to win prizes?'

The boys' conversation was interrupted by a familiar screech. 'HALT!' they heard from the reception area. As the gang turned around, they saw Ms O'Gorman striding towards them. She marched right up to Bushy and gave him a devastating glare. 'Are you telling me you sneaked a pet into my hotel without telling me?'

Bushy gawped at her, trying to get his bearings. 'I – I didn't realise pets weren't allowed.'

'They aren't,' Ms O'Gorman said. But as she glanced down at Wilbur, all the intense energy inside her seemed to vanish. 'But I make an exception for rabbits. I mean, look at this little fella. He's adorable!'

Bushy couldn't believe what he was hearing. He was taken aback already by David being nice about Wilbur, but he'd never expected the hotel manager would react this way. 'D-do you want to hold him?'

Ms O'Gorman's face lit up. 'Can I?'

'Yeah, just be careful. He had a long day at the pet show.'

Ms O'Gorman gently lifted him into her arms and stroked him slowly. 'And I heard you won as well,' she said, like she was talking to a baby. 'Of course you won, you little munchkin!'

Declan and Stewy gave each other a funny look. Ms O'Gorman was acting so affectionate, it was like they were looking at a different person. Based on their earlier run-in with her, they never would have pictured Ms O'Gorman acting this way.

'He looks so fluffy,' Big Mike said. 'Can I touch hi–?'

Ms O'Gorman held up a firm hand. 'I'm petting him,' she said sternly.

'One at a time, guys!' Bushy said, trying to take control of the situation. 'You'll all have a chance to pet him.'

Not only did the whole experience boost Bushy's confidence, but it also helped them to stay positive for what was coming: playing against Tyrone.

* * *

The following morning, they had an early breakfast and then packed up all their stuff before getting on the bus. This was going to be their last day at the hotel, regardless of the result. They were either going to be heading to Croke Park or their journey would be finished. The semi-final was going to push them to the limit. When the bus pulled out, the boys could see Ms O'Gorman waving goodbye.

As they drove to the pitch, Declan felt like his mind should be focused on the match. Yet he couldn't help thinking about home. Even though they were having a great time at the tournament, he was feeling homesick. It wasn't easy playing matches almost every day.

At the same time, he knew he should devote all his attention to this match. It wasn't fair to the other players to be unfocused. He had to appreciate the opportunity Brendan had given him. Brendan was tough but he was always fair. He'd got angry after the first night, but that was justified. He was generous, giving them time each day to spend in Salthill. He'd even lent one or two of the lads a few euro when they overspent.

What Brendan didn't know was that the team had decided to chip in and buy him a leather wallet. Whether they won or lost against Tyrone, they thought after the match would be a good time to give it to him. They'd also bought a tie for the bus driver, Paddy. Bushy had used his winnings to buy the tie himself.

When the boys arrived, they got set up in the dressing room. When Brendan came in his hands were clenched and there was a serious look on his face. Billy was out for this one. He still hadn't recovered from food poisoning. It was clear that the pressure was on. 'Right, lads, there isn't that much opportunity to play in Croke Park at your age, and there are many, many fine footballers who never get to play in Croke Park at all. That should be enough motivation. I want you to go out there and give everything you've got. Tyrone won their last match by six points and they're now favourites for the competition.'

Bushy, Stewy and the rest naturally assumed Brendan was getting stressed because they were getting closer and closer to the final. But Declan thought it was something deeper than that. Since only one of the thirty-two teams could win, perhaps Brendan hadn't expected they'd make it this far. If they lost, it wouldn't be a surprise. After all, only one team could win the All-Ireland. But now they were in the semi-final, Brendan was thinking it was very possible they could win. Nobody had expected much out of them.

But then again, they were about to play the team expected to win. Being positive wasn't going to be enough to beat them. They couldn't underestimate Tyrone for a second.

As soon as the game began, they got a good start. Stewy blazed down the wing and fired the ball over the bar, earning the first point. Brian Bohan caught the next kick-out and ran through from midfield to score a point himself. Declan could hear the roars of the crowd urging them on.

But this Tyrone team were favourites to win for a reason, and they soon got into their stride. Their centre-forward was clearly their secret weapon. Despite his bulky size, he was lightning fast. He was winning lots of ball around the middle, and while he wasn't getting on the scoreboard himself, he was helping his teammates get points. After 20 minutes, Tyrone were winning 0–8 to 0–4, with their centre-forward having a hand in six of those points.

But just as the half-time whistle was about to be blown, Declan managed to intercept a hand-pass from their wing-back. He was already sprinting at full tilt when he caught the ball. With that momentum, he managed to evade their full-back. Just before their keeper came to smother him, he popped the ball out to the inrushing David Jenkins, who slotted the ball into an empty net.

Immediately after that, the referee blew his whistle. Tyrone were still ahead, but now Declan's team had a lifeline. They were only a point behind, and the goal just before half-time gave them new hope.

During the break, there was no messing around. Brendan didn't have to say much. They knew what they had to do. They were at a point where they had to give it their all – nothing else would be good enough.

Tyrone

Everyone to a man played much better in the second half and they slowly began to turn the tide against Tyrone. David Jenkins popped over a free kick, Declan swung over a point from play, and Jack Maher created a goal for Cathal Hayes with one of those diagonal balls.

With five minutes left, they were winning by two points. In most of their matches, they'd won with a last-minute point or goal. This time, they were already winning and they had to do everything in their power to keep the opposition at bay. If they scored a single goal, it was over. Knowing that victory was near, Tyrone gave it everything they had in those last few minutes.

Their centre-forward boomed over a point from way out, then caught the next kick-out and raced through the middle, popped it off to their corner-forward, who smashed his shot off the crossbar, knocking it back out. If it had been an inch lower, that goal would have spelled doom for Declan's team.

They were exhausted and Tyrone seemed to be winning every kick-out and every fifty-fifty.

Their wing-forward had a chance to level it but his shot went narrowly wide.

'Time must be up, ref,' Declan shouted desperately. He usually said nothing to the referee but there was so much riding on this match. A chance to play at Croke Park meant everything to him. The referee dismissed him with a wave of his hand.

As Tyrone lofted their next attack into the box, Bushy came out, managed to avoid the full-forward's fierce attempt to jostle him and kicked the ball out to Jack Maher. Eager to get the ball up the field as quickly as possible, Jack hit a long pass up to the full-forward line. With that, they heard the referee's whistle, confirming their victory. Instead of cheering and high-fiving each other, they fell to their knees in exhaustion, knowing that the next match would somehow be tougher.

Tyrone

FINAL SCORE

2-10
0-15

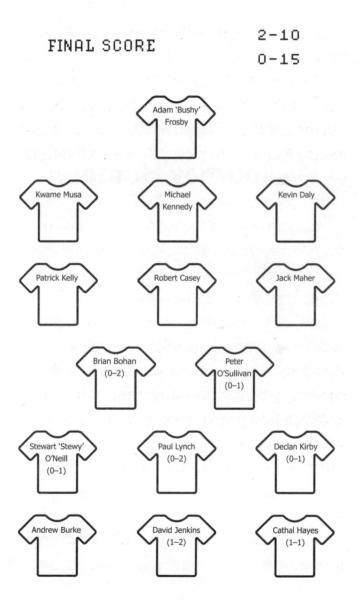

Adam 'Bushy' Frosby

Kwame Musa

Michael Kennedy

Kevin Daly

Patrick Kelly

Robert Casey

Jack Maher

Brian Bohan (0–2)

Peter O'Sullivan (0–1)

Stewart 'Stewy' O'Neill (0–1)

Paul Lynch (0–2)

Declan Kirby (0–1)

Andrew Burke

David Jenkins (1–2)

Cathal Hayes (1–1)

Chapter 19

Journey Home

When the celebrations had settled down, Brendan told the team that the final would be against Kerry. Declan wasn't that surprised, given their history of getting to finals.

They waited until they were all on the bus before they presented Brendan with the wallet. At first, he didn't realise it was a gift. He thought they'd found a lost wallet and were giving it to him for safekeeping. Only when he opened it and saw that it was empty did he understand that they'd bought it for him. As he chuckled to himself, he held up his present high and proud. 'There won't be any money to put in this if I have to keep taking you lads out to celebrate,' he joked. They all laughed and cheered.

Declan made his way towards him. 'Brendan, even if we lose the next game, we just want you to know we wouldn't be here without you. Thanks for making this a great trip.'

'Thank you very much ... captain,' he said.

As happy as Brendan was with his gift, it was nothing compared to how chuffed Paddy was when they presented him with the tie. Of course, it was Bushy who did the honours on that occasion. 'Just want to say thanks for driving us around and for minding Wilbur. If it wasn't for you, he wouldn't have won the rabbit show.'

'Aw, thanks a million,' Paddy said softly. He was so taken aback, it was like he had never received a gift before. As he opened the box Bushy had given him, he looked at the tie inside. Declan had thought Paddy would see it as a sweet little gift, but it clearly meant a lot to him, judging by the beaming smile on his face. Then he stood up and turned to the boys, suddenly looking surprisingly angry. 'What's all this nonsense about "if we lose"? What are ya on about? I'm in the presence of the future champions of Ireland!' he said, a smile breaking out on his face.

Paddy's inspiring words caused them all to burst into cheers. The boys at the back began chanting and singing. Everyone was in such good spirits that Brendan let them carry on for a few minutes before he eventually stood up, waved his hand and said, 'Right, lads, that's enough. I don't want to be hearing that all the way home.'

Declan tried to keep his eyes open but he was so tired after the game that he nodded off within a few minutes. The next time he opened his eyes, he looked out the window and noticed that they were in Dublin. Sleepy as he was, he had to nudge Stewy to wake him

up. Despite the noise continuing at the back of
the bus, he had dozed off, as had several other
players. The game had obviously taken its toll
on them. They were all aching after playing
such a hard match and they needed to be in
tip-top shape for the final in two days' time. It
was a shame they had so little time to heal. A
week of relaxing would have been ideal, but
Declan knew that wasn't going to happen.

He noticed Brendan standing at the front of
the bus with his hand up – it looked like he had
something important to say.

'While some of you guys were sleeping, I
managed to organise a hotel for us close to
Croke Park and arrange for us to visit Croker
tomorrow for a quick tour, so hopefully that will
settle you down before our game on Saturday.'

Stewy and Declan just looked at each other,
speechless. It was really happening. Croke
Park. The big time.

Chapter 20

Croke Park

For some people, the most beautiful building in the world is the Taj Mahal or the Eiffel Tower. But for Declan, it would always be Croke Park. Even though he'd been there countless times, it still blew him away.

'You ready, guys?' Brendan asked. 'This place is the biggest stadium in Ireland – third largest in Europe. I don't want anyone to get lost before tomorrow's game so I'll walk you through how to get to our changing room.'

Croke Park

As they walked in, Declan could hear all the players whispering to each other.

'I heard it's named after an archbishop or something.'

'Didn't the pope come here?'

'Saw a hurling match here last year.'

Every now and again, Stewy would nudge Declan to get his attention and point out a plaque or a trophy or a photograph. He'd then explain the significance behind it. But Declan wasn't really listening. He didn't need Stewy to tell him anything because he knew it all. He knew about the Hogan Stand and how the stadium once hosted the Special Olympics. The Olympic torch itself was brought there in 2012.

He knew a lot of people on the team probably felt the same way, but he genuinely believed he knew more than anyone about Croke Park. He knew when it was built and that it could hold over 80,000 people. And now he was actually going to play there.

As he looked into the distance, he saw someone studying one of the medals on display. It took him a second to recognise him. 'Harry?'

'Huh?' As Harry turned around, he looked just as surprised to see Declan as Declan was to see him. 'Dec!'

'Y-you're here!' he gasped. After Harry had left for Poland, Declan hadn't expected to see him again any time soon. 'W-what are you doing here?'

'Did you actually think I'd miss you guys playing in the final?' he asked. 'I couldn't play with you, but there was no way I wasn't going to see you.'

'We? Are your family here too?'

Before Harry had a chance to answer, Declan felt a big hand clasp his shoulder and swing him around. 'Dereck!' he yelled. He looked down to see that Dereck was still wearing a metal boot on his broken ankle. 'Still hasn't healed fully, has it?'

'I'm off the crutches, though,' Dereck said. 'Thank god. Getting in here tomorrow with crutches would be a nightmare!'

By this point, Bushy and Stewy had seen Harry and Dereck and came over. 'Wow, guys!' Bushy shouted. 'What a surprise to see you!'

'It was meant to be a surprise,' Dereck said, disappointed. 'We didn't want to put you guys under any pressure so we all decided not to tell you we were all coming.'

'Who's "all"?' Stewy asked. 'There's only two of you.'

Dereck had that smirk on his face he always had when he had a secret. 'He can tell you himself,' he said, gesturing behind them.

Declan turned around and gasped to see Sam. 'You're here too!'

'I'm so proud of you guys!' Sam said, smiling.

'Dec, I've only been back for a few hours,' Harry said. 'But everyone is talking about the match.'

'Really?' Stewy and Declan said in unison.

'Don't act so surprised,' Sam said. 'Everyone's dying to see you guys playing in Croker. You've captured the heart of the county.'

'Yeah,' Declan said uncertainly. 'Now all we have to do is win.'

Chapter 21

The Big One

Before Declan went to bed, he gave his mum a call. He was a bag of nerves and knew talking to her would calm him down.

After two rings, he heard her reassuring voice. 'Hi, sweetie,' she said.

'Hey, Mum,' he said, trying to stay calm.

'Big day tomorrow. Dad and I can't wait to see you play.'

'Yeah,' he said, laughing nervously. 'I'm freaking out a bit.'

The Big One

'You always do when you're passionate about something. It's not necessarily a bad thing. I mean, you were stressed about the county final and look how that turned out!'

'Thanks, Mum,' he said. 'Any tips from Granddad?'

'He says you don't need any more advice from him,' she said. 'You know all you need to know, Declan. Win or lose, I know you'll play your best.'

'Thanks, Mum.' A moment before, Declan's heart had been pounding like crazy. After speaking to his mum for a few seconds, he already felt calmer. She always had that effect on him. 'I'm going to need my rest for the big game, so I'll talk to you tomorrow.'

'Night, sweetie,' she said. As he hung up, he no longer felt worried. He was buzzing. In fact, Declan thought he wouldn't sleep out of excitement, but he was out like a light the second his head hit the pillow. His body seemed to know it needed him to be fully energised for the big day.

It didn't take long to get to Croke Park, but it felt like an eternity. When the team did arrive, the building was already littered with hundreds of people. As they headed into the stadium, Declan could see that plenty of people from Kerry had made the journey up, as he spotted lots of groups in green and gold jerseys.

The changing rooms were amazing. As well as a central space, each player had their own cubicle where they got changed. Declan had never had that before. He felt like a celebrity.

By this point, Billy Graham was feeling OK again and was able to play. When Brendan told Declan this, he assumed he would step down as captain and Billy would take the position again. But Brendan believed Declan had proved himself to the team and said he should still lead the lads. Billy didn't mind – he was just happy to be well enough to play in the final. Declan felt honoured but he knew he couldn't get carried away: he needed to focus on the game.

Brendan stepped forward into the centre of the dressing room.

The Big One

'Lads, nobody expected us to be here but you did everything we asked of you. You listened to the advice we gave you, you worked hard for each other, and we never gave up even when things went against us. But this is our biggest challenge, playing against one of the best teams in the country. But you know what? I believe in you guys. You have to believe it too – go out there and give it everything you have and see what happens! I believe in every one of you!'

With Brendan's words ringing in their ears, they ran onto the pitch with pep in their step. Declan noticed how soft the grass felt. *Croke Park is so amazing, even the grass is better!*, he thought. As he looked at the crowd, the nerves finally kicked in. He knew the fear would get to him at some point. He said to himself, over and over, *I want this. I want it so bad. I am where I wanted to be more than anything, and I want to stay here as long as I can.*

Dereck and Harry weren't kidding. There were at least 500 people at the match. Declan couldn't even spot where his mum and dad were. But it didn't matter that he couldn't see them: he knew they were there. Although the stadium could fit far more, it was the biggest crowd Declan had ever played to.

As the Kerry team entered the pitch, he felt a second wave of jitters travel through his body, giving him goosebumps galore. When you know you can lose the one thing you want more than anything, it's normal to be scared.

He had to push through it. It was like what his granddad said about Jesse Owens: don't make excuses. He didn't have time or a place to train, so he trained mentally. Mind over matter. Declan knew he could push through the anxiety with willpower. He just hoped that was enough to become the All-Ireland champions.

The referee called for the captains so Declan walked up towards the centre of the pitch. He shook hands with the Kerry captain, who was about a foot taller than him!

The referee looked at Declan. 'OK, call it – what'll it be, heads or tails?'

The Big One

'Heads,' Declan said.

The ref quickly flicked the coin. 'Heads it is.'

'We'll play with the wind,' Declan said.

'OK, no problem. Tell your team to get into their positions. Best of luck to both of you.'

Declan jogged over to his wing, taking another look at the crowd. The wing-back had a look of determination on his face as they shook hands. This is it, Declan thought. Here we go!

When the referee threw up the ball, one of the Kerry midfielders caught it cleanly and lamped it in to their full-forward. Big Mike rose to the clouds and fetched the ball out of the air, laying off a hand-pass to Billy Graham. Billy spotted Stewy and delivered a beautifully accurate pass straight in to his chest. *There could be something on for me here*, Declan thought as he sped forward. He remembered his grandfather's words about always making the run. Stewy was soloing up the field but there was a back coming straight for him.

'Stewy,' Declan shouted just before the back got to him. He laid the ball off and Declan collected it at full speed to rifle it high over the bar for the perfect start. He breathed a sigh of relief and quickly began to feel more confident. He'd just scored a point in an All-Ireland final! No matter how the game went, no one could take that away from him. He had nothing to lose now. He settled down and actually started to enjoy the game. And the more he enjoyed it, the less stressed he felt, which actually allowed him to play better.

This was the game of their lives, so everyone was giving 100 per cent. David was zipping around the opposition like a machine. Billy was so quick with the ball, you wouldn't believe he'd been bedridden two days ago. Stewy was moving so fast, it seemed he couldn't run out of energy. Paul and David played off each other so well – it was like they were sharing one mind. Even though Declan was in the heat of the game, he felt so proud to be part of such a great team.

He was giving his all. He really was. With the sun beating down and him galloping around the pitch like a gazelle, he was sweating buckets. He had never been so tired in his life. And they weren't even through the first half of the game!

He didn't have a choice. He had to push through it. It was tough because Kerry's defence was hard to break down. They defended superbly and often had one of their midfielders back to help out. Their strategy seemed to be very simple: they wouldn't give an inch. They made few mistakes and misplaced very few balls. Any time Declan's team got the ball, Kerry got it back. When Kerry got the ball, Declan's team got it back. Their skills were so even, it was like they were cancelling each other out. By the time the ref blew the whistle for half-time, it was five points each.

Chapter 22

Our Moment

Kerry were so good, it was a challenge to get a single point. Declan's team had to be better to turn this around. As he looked at his teammates, he could see that they had used up most of their energy. He jogged up to Stewy, who was bent over and wincing in pain.

'What's wrong?' he asked.

'Stitch,' Stewy said, clenching his teeth.

'You have to rest,' Declan warned him. 'You're no help to anyone if that doesn't go away.'

'I'm more tired now than I thought I would be at the end of the match,' Stewy panted, looking defeated. 'And we still have the second half! What are we going to do?'

'There's only one thing we can do,' Declan said. 'Wait for them to make a mistake. They're a great team … but they're still human. It just takes one player to slip or stumble, and BAM! We need to be on it.'

'And what if they don't make a mistake?'

'Then we lose, knowing we did our best.'

'Yeah, you're right,' Stewy said, starting to get his breath back. 'And you know what, win or lose, we played at Croke Park. How many people can say they've done that?'

'Guys,' Jack Maher yelled. 'The ref's coming back on. Get ready.'

When the whistle blew for the second half, Brian Bohan lofted a ball in towards David Jenkins at full-forward but it was slightly too high to catch. Declan ran in towards the full-forward line and heard David shouting his name. He anticipated what he was going to do. David palmed the ball towards Declan and he collected it. He sprinted as fast as he could, then the goalkeeper came out, narrowing the angle, so Declan hand-passed the ball over the bar. However, as he veered to the right to avoid a collision with the keeper, he was still going at full tilt and smacked his shoulder off the goalpost.

It took everything he had to get back on his feet. He tried his best to ignore the throbbing pain in his shoulder.

'DECLAN!' Stewy roared as he ran towards him. 'Are you OK?'

'I – I think so,' he said unsurely.

'Wait!' Brendan shouted as he made his way onto the pitch. 'Are you hurt, Declan?'

'Yes, but I'm fine,' he said, doing his best to mask the pain.

'Can you continue to play?' the referee asked him.

'What?'

'Look, Declan,' Brendan said. 'I can't have you playing if you've injured yourself – you could do some serious damage to your shoulder. I can't risk that. If you feel like you can't play your best, you should come off and I'll send someone else on. No one will think less of you.'

Declan felt a lump in his throat. He was in pain but he was doing everything in his power to mask it. He wanted to keep playing. He needed to. But at the same time, if he couldn't move well, he would be risking his team's chance of winning for the sake of his own pride.

'Can you carry on?' the referee asked.

He took a moment to really think about it. *Do I just bow out and trust my teammates to play? I should only continue if I truly think I'll help the team and not drag them down.* He knew losing was likely, but it would kill him if they lost because of his screw-up.

But then again, Brendan had made him captain because he thought Declan had potential. And a true captain doesn't bail at the first sign of trouble. His shoulder was really sore, but he had to downplay it, otherwise Brendan would take him off.

'I was dazed for a second but I'm fine now,' he reassured them. 'It was the shock of it more than anything. Caught me by surprise.'

'OK,' the ref said. The Kerry goalkeeper kicked out the ball towards the middle of the field. Brian Bohan managed to catch it but he didn't see two players coming in from behind. When he finally noticed, he instinctively kicked it to Declan, since he was the only one nearby. Because Declan had just been injured, no one was marking him, which gave him plenty of time with the ball. As he got closer to the goal, he saw their massive full-back striding towards him at full pace. As Declan bounced the ball he felt a sharp pain dart up his shoulder, but he had to keep going – this was it, no giving up now.

As the full-back grew nearer and nearer, Declan realised he had to take a chance. He blasted the ball and smashed it into the back of the net.

First goal of the game! Their supporters went nuts. Since the crowd was ten times larger than anything he'd ever played in front of, it was literally the loudest sound he'd ever heard as a player. And it was all for them. It was an amazing feeling ... but they hadn't won yet.

His teammates dashed towards him and Big Mike lifted him in the air and spun him around. Then David grabbed him and gave him a high five. 'You scared me like crazy! I thought you were going to have to go off a few minutes ago. You genius, you!'

As they continued playing, it was like each player had a second wind. Since they were a goal ahead, it would be understandable if they wanted to take it easy. They were all exhausted and everyone was desperate to take a breather. But if they took it easy, even for a second, it would be enough time for Kerry to get the ball past them. Catching their breath for a moment could be the difference between winning and losing. They had to push on.

Kerry were catching up gradually, relying on scoring points. They weren't trying for goals, deeming it too risky. However, every time they got a point, Declan's team managed to get one back.

With ten minutes left on the clock, Kerry adjusted their game plan. They were five down, 0–8 to 1–10. They didn't have a chance of winning if they kept going for points. They needed goals.

The odds seemed to be stacked against them, but Kerry were a resilient bunch, and their centre-back threw caution to the wind by powering forward after he caught a kick-out. He played a one-two with his full-forward before smashing the ball to the back of the net from 20 metres out.

Declan's team were now only two up, 1–10 to 1–8. If Kerry scored one more goal, they would win by a single point. In the county final, Declan had scored the winning goal for his club, Smithgreen, in the last few minutes. Now the shoe was on the other foot. His team were winning and they had to do everything they could to stop the opposition from reaching that goal. But this was their moment. In 300 seconds, it would all be over and they would see who'd emerge victorious.

Our Moment

Stewy kicked a sideline ball in to Cathal Hayes. Declan was on the outside. Cathal popped it over to him and Declan made a mad dash with the ball. His legs were aching at this point but he didn't care. They were too close to victory for him to do anything except give it his all. As his calves started cramping, he tried to push through it. He only had to be strong for a few minutes. The game would be over before he knew it.

As he tried to kick it towards Brian Bohan, the Kerry centre-back intercepted it and stormed up the field, delivering a pass just in front of their full-forward who laid it off to one of their midfielders running through. As Declan raced after him, he could see he was about to take a shot. In a last-ditch effort, Declan tried to knock the ball out of his hands but missed. Seeing him approach, the Kerry midfielder rushed the shot and blasted the ball full force. He hit it with such ferocity, Declan knew Bushy didn't have a chance of catching it. Even if he did, the force would knock him into the back of the net.

As he helplessly saw the ball sail towards the goal, Declan could see it was going for the top-right corner. Even the best goalkeeper could never reach that high. The ball was airborne for about two seconds but it felt like it was frozen in time – this shot would decide everything.

Then they all heard an echoing clang as the ball smashed off the bar before sailing over for a point.

'OHHHHH!' Every player on the field and every person in the crowd made the exact same sound – relief from their supporters and anguish from the Kerry fans.

With that point, the score had Declan's team still winning 1–10 to 1–9. Thank god that hadn't happened sooner, he thought. It felt like his legs were turning to jelly.

After less than a minute, he heard the sweetest sound in the world: the final whistle.

It was over. They'd done it. Champions. As soon as Declan heard the whistle, he felt a sudden sharp pain in his shoulder. It was like he'd been holding back the pain through pure willpower, and now that the game was over, he was feeling the full force of the injury.

But he didn't care. No pain could cancel out the sheer joy he felt. He dropped to his knees and screamed into the sky. 'YESSSSS!' he yelled as loudly as he could. Bushy, Big Mike and the rest of them jumped on him and started rolling around on the ground. He could hear everyone in the crowd chanting, clapping and stamping their feet. He swore he could feel their thunderous applause shaking the ground. As he got to his feet, he felt somebody clap him on the back. It was his mum and dad. 'Well done, son,' his dad said. Declan then noticed his brother, Daniel. 'Way to go, Dec!' he cried. Behind him, his sister, Louise, appeared. 'OK, you know football isn't my thing, but that was pretty awesome to watch,' she said smiling.

Just then, Declan saw an official talking to Brendan, who then beckoned them over towards the Hogan Stand.

Wow. They were going up to the podium. As they walked up, Declan realised he'd barely rehearsed a speech. He'd only been thinking about the game. As they gathered on the steps, an official took the microphone.

'What a wonderful way to end this first underage competition, with a terrific final played in an honest, sporting manner. The two teams are a credit to their counties, their mentors and their families. I will now present the cup to the captain of the winning team, Declan Kirby.'

Just before Declan took a step forward, a thought went through his head. Billy. He turned to see that he was halfway down the steps. 'Billy,' he cried out.

'What?'

'I want you to lift the cup with me.' Declan noticed the look of astonishment on his face as he slowly made his way up, carefully pushing through the rest of the lads. He then approached Declan, and that look had changed to a big smile.

'Thanks for this. I wasn't expecting it at all.'

'No problem, Billy. You earned it. Now let's raise it high.'

With that, the two of them lofted the cup into the air, looking out on the hundreds of supporters who were cheering and clapping wildly.

Declan then took the microphone.

'Tá an-áthas orm an corn seo a ghlacadh ar son na foirne iontaí seo. I would like to thank Kerry for a great sporting game. They are an amazing team with an amazing tradition. I want to thank all of our supporters who came here today. Who would have thought when we started out on this journey that we would end up in Croke Park?

'Many of you followed us up to Galway, where we won some matches by the skin of our teeth, and it was your support and encouragement that helped us get here today. When the game was in the balance there, in the last few minutes, you helped to get us over the line. Thank you so much.

'Finally, I want to thank a legend in our county – he was a great footballer himself and he decided to take us on to help our football development. He's been brilliant and we hope to be like him one day. Brendan Kelly, thank you so much!'

The team and their supporters clapped and cheered. Declan lifted the cup one more time to another cheer from the crowd. Before he passed the cup along the line to the rest of the lads, he took one last look out onto the field, their supporters waving their flags, tears of joy on some people's faces, on the greatest pitch of them all. It couldn't get better than this.

Our Moment

FINAL SCORE

1-10
1-9

Adam 'Bushy' Frosby

Kwame Musa

Michael Kennedy

Kevin Daly

Patrick Kelly

Billy Graham

Jack Maher

Brian Bohan (0–1)

Peter O'Sullivan (0–1)

Stewart 'Stewy' O'Neill (0–1)

Paul Lynch (0–2)

Declan Kirby (1–2)

Andrew Burke

David Jenkins (0–2)

Cathal Hayes (0–1)

Preview for *GAA Star:*
Back of the Net

Chapter 1

The New Teacher

It felt weird to Declan to be back in school. Since he'd taken part in the underage All-Ireland Gaelic football competition during the summer, it had felt like he'd barely had any time off. He was so exhausted after all those matches, he felt like he needed a month of sleep. But only two weeks after his team won the tournament, he was starting sixth class. It felt like the shortest summer ever!

As soon as he walked into the classroom, his best friend, Stewy, was there to greet him.

Since he'd played with Stewy all summer, it was weird to see him wearing a school uniform instead of a jersey.

'You alright?' Stewy said.

'Grand – good to see you,' Declan said, sitting down at the desk beside him.

'Hey, man,' Big Mike said from behind. 'Did you have a good summer? Well, what was left of it, I mean.'

'Yeah, it felt like we had a week off!'

'It is annoying,' Stewy said, 'but look on the bright side. Do you know who we won't have to see anymore?'

'Eh, no. Who?'

'Ms Murphy!' he said. He was so excited, he practically squealed.

'Oh, yeah!' Big Mike said, breathing a sigh of relief. 'Well, she's not gone completely. She's just teaching in the other prefab.'

'That means we have Mrs Healy,' Declan reminded them. 'All the old students said she's dead sound. She makes you work hard but she's fair. Never raises her voice unless someone actually deserves it. Unlike Ms Murphy. I don't think there was ever a time where she didn't roar at us.'

'Em … guys,' someone said behind them. Declan turned around to see Séamus. Although he had been in Declan's class for years, he didn't know him that well. He seemed like a nice guy but he didn't play football, so Declan never had much chance to speak to him.

'Don't mean to interrupt you, but were you just talking about Mrs Healy?'

'Yeah,' Declan said. 'Why?'

'Did you not hear?'

'Hear what?'

'She left the school,' Séamus said. 'Got a job somewhere else. We have a new teacher.'

'What? Seriously?' Stewy said. 'Why did the best teacher have to leave? Why didn't this happen with Ms Murphy last year?'

'Relax,' Declan said. 'We don't know anything about this teacher. Séamus, do you know who it is?'

'Yeah.' He nodded. 'Mr O'Flaherty.'

'Heh!' Big Mike sniggered. 'Same name as that crazy coach.'

'Em, yeah. That's our new teacher.'

'WHAT!' Stewy yelled. 'I heard that guy was nuts!'

'How do you know about this?' Declan asked Séamus.

'My dad knows him and he mentioned he was taking over for Mrs Healy. And he's not crazy. He's just … passionate. He really, really, really likes sports. Like, a lot.'

'I didn't even know he taught,' Big Mike said. 'I mean … can he?'

'Guys, you'll be fine,' Séamus reassured them. 'Mr O'Flaherty is great. Just behave and you'll have nothing to worry about. And don't speak out of turn. Or too loud. Or too quiet. And don't interrupt him. He hates that. Oh, and don't look him right in the eye.'

'This guy sounds scarier than Ms Murphy,' Stewy said.

'Get to your seats!' a voice barked from the door. And in marched Mr O'Flaherty. A giant

The New Teacher

of a man, his head almost touched the door
frame as he entered the room.

The chatter stopped in an instant and
the students all dived to their desks. Mr
O'Flaherty took a moment to scan them all. Oh,
wow, Declan thought. Séamus wasn't kidding.
His eyes were so piercing, like a falcon seeking
its prey.

Their new teacher then took a big step
forward, his huge frame nearly eclipsing the
whole whiteboard, the ground underneath him
almost quaking.

Then he opened his mouth and started
belting out the national anthem.

'Sinne Fianna Fáil

Atá faoi gheall ag Éirinn ...'

Declan and Stewy exchanged puzzled looks
before the whole class joined in, trying their
best to sing it perfectly. If they made a mistake
or forgot a part, they might suffer the fury
of this Mr O'Flaherty. Declan would have this
teacher for the rest of the year, so he needed
to make a good first impression.

When they finished, Mr O'Flaherty gave the class another piercing stare. 'English books. Out. Now.'

Usually, a new teacher would introduce themselves and ask the students to talk about themselves a little bit. There was none of that with this guy. He was all business. As the class worked through their books, no one dared misbehave or talk back.

When the bell rang, the class headed out for their first break. As Declan was about to go out the door, Mr O'Flaherty stopped him dead. 'Declan Kirby!' he yelled, pointing to him.

'Y-yeah?' Declan said nervously. *What did I do wrong*? he thought. He didn't speak to me for the whole class.

'I want a word with you,' Mr O'Flaherty said, fixing him with his eyes. 'You and I need to have a very serious chat.'